FLOOD TIDE

Reah Lawrence has been haunted by an unknown man in a terrifying dream ever since the death of her father, a famous yachtsman. When Ewart Morgan, a successful television playwright, arrives to give the end of term lecture at the school where Reah teaches art, she recognises him instantly as the man in her nightmare.

In Florence their tempestuous romance blossoms, despite an amorous Italian and a beautiful Contessa who almost destroy the magic. Back on the stormy Sussex coast, Reah finally finds the answer to her disturbing dream.

FLOOD TIDE

Flood Tide

by
Stella Whitelaw

Dales Large Print Books
Long Preston, North Yorkshire,
England.

British Library Cataloguing in Publication Data.

Whitelaw, Stella
  Flood tide.

  A catalogue record for this book is
  available from the British Library

  ISBN 1-85389-814-7 pbk

First published in Great Britain by Robert Hale Ltd., 1986

Copyright © 1986 by Stella Whitelaw

Cover illustration © Hancock by arrangement with Allied
Artists

The moral right of the author has been asserted

Published in Large Print 1998 by arrangement with Stella
Whitelaw

Dales Large Print is an imprint of
Library Magna Books Ltd.
Printed and bound in Great Britain by
T.J. International Ltd., Cornwall, PL28 8RW.

To

Swanwick Writers' Conference
where this story began

ONE

Later she could not remember why she had been in such a hurry that morning, her head in a book.

It had been an old rust coloured leather-bound book she had picked up at Oxborough market, the pages brown-edged and fragile, the faded printing difficult to read and the pen-drawn illustrations like spider's legs on the paper.

She had been hurrying along the main corridor at college, absorbed in the old book, when some small spine-chilling message made her look up instinctively.

The staircase at Oxborough College was a curving sweep of wide, worn oak treads, a relic of the days when the main building had been the home of a prosperous Victorian coal baron.

She stopped at the foot of the stairs. A swift sense of apprehension ran through her veins. She stood, staring, frozen to the spot.

There was a man on the stairs. He was descending the long sweep with an easy vitality that drew her gaze like a magnet. He was quite tall, wearing a casual pale blue safari suit and an open-necked blue shirt. His light brown hair was cropped Hamlet-style with a fringe falling over his tanned brow.

But it was his eyes which drew and held Reah's gaze. They were the most electrifying dark brown eyes she had ever seen; laughter crinkles at the corners like fans of sunshine on his tanned skin.

She stood, rooted, the book still open in her hand.

'Are you about to say something important?' he said briskly. 'If not, young lady, would you kindly get out of my way?'

The accent was difficult to place. Later Reah was to know that it was Welsh, nurtured in a tiny village tucked in the green hills where Ewart Morgan had grown up and become a man who wrote magic onto the television screen with an ease that belied the lonely hours of discipline and concentration behind every play.

'Sorry. I'm s—sorry,' she stammered, unable to move.

His eyes raked over her. He was taking in the old Trilby hat crammed down on her red hair; the tight patched jeans; the baggy sweater that hid the femininity of her figure. Amusement, then irritation flashed through his expressive brown eyes.

'If you're going, then go—if not, perhaps I could climb over you?' he suggested, his voice now tinged with exasperation. 'No doubt this habit of blocking the stairs always makes you late for your class.'

He thought she was a student. Reah was not surprised. She looked about sixteen with her fine-boned face freshly scrubbed and her mane of red hair tucked up under the old Trilby. She loved the old hat. It had been one of her father's. It made her feel close to him, wearing his old hat. It was his sweater too, a baggy cable knit which her aunt had produced for him to wear on his sailing boat. He had not been wearing it the day the boat overturned during a sudden squall off the coast. The lifeboat crew had searched for his body for hours. He had been washed up on deserted French sand dunes days later, sea-battered and hardly recognisable. It had not helped that the sailing boat had been called 'Reah'.

The man on the stairs made as if to squeeze past her. Reah moved in the same direction. It was like a farce, predictable comedy from a sit-com.

'Since you are obviously intent on preventing me from being on time for my lecture, perhaps I'd better start climbing now?' he said. 'I take it you are on your way to the conference hall?'

Reah shook her head, the Trilby tipping a little over her eyes. She guessed he must be the visiting celebrity come to give the end of term lecture. Ewart Morgan, the playwright.

Miss Hardcastle, headmistress of Oxborough College, expected Reah, as the youngest member of staff, to make the customary speech of thanks, but Reah hated having to do it.

That was why she was not going to the Ewart Morgan lecture.

'No,' she said, looking him firmly in the eye, those penetratingly deep eyes which were still taking her apart. 'I don't go on ego-trips.'

Her words cut through the air and hung there as if she had spray-painted them on the walls. She heard his sharp intake of breath. In his left hand he was holding a stick.

It was a thin bent branch of silver birch. He had picked it in the grounds of the college to use as a pointer for the black board in the conference hall.

'What a pity,' he said, the ice edge to his voice telling Reah that she had gone too far, much too far. 'You might have learned some good manners.'

He touched her sharply on the arm with the stick. She felt the rap shoot along the raw nerve ends of her arm. It was almost a pain and she had to bite her lip to stop herself crying out.

Ewart Morgan brushed past her. He was taller than she had thought; her eyes were level with his shoulder. He was very slim, the leather belt round his flat waist fastened on the last hole. She was taking in everything about him; her mind was acting like a camera.

He strode away down the corridor and she watched his back, memorising in every detail, seeing the controlled vitality in his walk and the set of his shoulders.

She would know him again. She already knew him. She had seen him before. But not on the stairs or anywhere. It had been in a dream. She had seen him in a dream that had been so frightening that for months she had shut it completely from her mind.

In one moment she had learned two devastating truths. The man in her dream had always been unknown. Now she could give the face a name. Ewart Morgan who had brought her so much distress when her father died. She turned blindly, pushing the thoughts away.

Reah fled up the back stairs to the high-windowed room where she taught art. She was shaking.

Staff were not supposed to make coffee in their rooms but Reah had an electric kettle in a cupboard. It was the last day of term and she could use the morning tidying the art room.

Oxborough College was not a top scale private school, though it had a good reputation for turning out nice young ladies. It was a haven where failed A and O level students could re-take their examinations after personal tuition.

Reah longed for the moment when she could start painting again.

Watercolour was her first love; pen and colour wash her second. She liked drawing buildings, finding surprises in every line and angle, every crevice and corner. She could touch a pen drawing with a wash so pale and delicate that the colour seemed more like a reflection.

Her father had always encouraged her to paint. She had painted everywhere from the age of four, including the bathroom walls, but he had forgiven her and the splodgy rainbows and fan-fingered men stayed on the walls till the next spate of re-decoration. If Reah had had a mother, things might have been different, but she had died soon after Reah's first birthday.

A wave of applause came from the conference hall. Then she heard the scrape of chairs on the floor. They were giving him a standing ovation. She imagined Ewart Morgan lapping up the teenage adulation, leaving the hall beside Miss Hardcastle, tapping his calf with the silver birch stick like a Regency buck.

She was leaning against the windowsill, sipping coffee when the door opened and Miss Hardcastle came in followed by the man Reah never wanted to see again. He looked at her with a flicker of curiosity.

'Ah, Reah, I thought I'd find you here,' said Miss Hardcastle. She turned to Ewart Morgan. 'May I introduce Reah Lawrence, our art teacher and the youngest member of my staff. Reah, I'm just showing our famous visitor round the college.'

Ewart inclined his head. 'We have already met,' he said. 'Though I was unaware that Miss Lawrence was on your teaching staff. I took her to be one of the students, a somewhat unorthodox student.'

Irene Hardcastle smiled. She was a tall woman with speckled brown hair in an out-of-date French pleat, and faded blue eyes behind half moon glasses. She had a great fondness for Reah and that was one reason for her latitude over Reah's casual appearance in class. Miss Hardcastle was also shrewd enough to know that Reah's trendy look took her a long way towards a good relationship with her pupils.

'Reah looks too young but I assure you she's fully qualified and a most responsible, diligent teacher.'

'Responsible and diligent enough to skip the end of term lecture?' he enquired, his eyes flashing a critical look across the room at Reah and the mug of coffee in her hand.

Miss Hardcastle held open the door. 'This is a lightning tour. Mr Morgan is due back in London for a script conference this afternoon,' she explained. 'Come and see me before you go, Reah.'

Ewart Morgan paused in the doorway,

his hands deep in his pockets, and rocked back on his heels.

'You've forgotten the still life,' he said, nodding towards a collection of over-ripe fruit on a plate. 'Unless you intend to make a study of the growth of mould.'

'That's not a still life,' said Reah, gathering her dignity. 'That is my lunch.'

The crinkle lines round his eyes deepened and he was laughing at her. She spun away, annoyed that he had managed to mock her again.

A few minutes later she saw him walking across the grass towards the tennis courts. She watched him, her artist's mind observing the movement of muscles in that long, determined stride. He would have a lovely body, she thought, lean and muscular and tanned. She stopped her thoughts abruptly in exasperation. She did not want to think about Ewart Morgan, ever. She did not want to acknowledge that there was anything special about the man. He was a sarcastic and arrogant cynic, and she certainly did not want to watch him drive away in an expensive and showy car.

There was the usual end of term noise and chaos. The girls eventually left the buildings, and Reah was able to lock the art room and go downstairs to Miss Hardcastle's study. She had taken off the Trilby hat and her long red hair hung round her shoulders, bouncy and vibrant.

'Well, Ewart Morgan seems to like you,' said Miss Hardcastle. 'He's left you a memento of his visit.'

She held out the silver birch stick. Reah could hardly believe her eyes. He could even insult her when he was miles away. It was unforgiveable.

'I take it that this is some kind of joke between you?'

'He may think it's funny but I find his humour quite pathetic.'

Miss Hardcastle decided to change the subject.

'Now, I really asked you to come and see me because I wanted to say how well you've done this term. I know how desperately you miss your father. It's been a difficult time for you, but you've coped admirably.'

'Thank you...'

Reah was suddenly back on the cliffs, staring into the uneasy seas, knowing with a chilling certainty that he would never return.

Miss Hardcastle was still talking...'and I do hope you are going to take a holiday. What are you planning to do?'

Reah dragged her mind back to the book-lined study.

'Holiday? Oh, nothing much. There are a lot of odd jobs to do around the cottage, and the garden has been terribly neglected this year. I might start painting again.'

'You really need a holiday. You ought to get away, have a change of scene.' Miss Hardcastle paused. Money was always a delicate matter. 'I hope we pay you enough salary for a little holiday?'

'Yes,' said Reah. 'I can afford to go away. And my father left me some money. I'm just not interested in holiday resorts or lazing about on a beach.'

Miss Hardcastle got up and came round the desk. She had a flat brown paper parcel in her hands.

'I've been turning out my bookcases at home. I've far too many books. I'll never read them all. You might like this one. It seems more your style.'

Reah took the parcel. It was a heavy book. A smile lit up her face. It was a long time since anyone had given her a present.

A smile quickly changed Reah's face. The remote beauty of the young woman's bones was suddenly brought into focus; the gentle, curving lips revealed lovely, even teeth; the large, wide-set hazel eyes sparkled with golden flecks like captured sunshine. It was altogether a radiantly dazzling smile.

'What a nice surprise. Thank you,' Reah said. 'Can I open it now?'

'No, wait until you get home. And send me a postcard.'

Reah smiled again. 'Thank you and good-bye till next term.'

'I wonder if you feel like doing me a

small favour before your holiday really starts?'

'Of course.'

'Would you show Ewart Morgan the short cut to the cliffs? He said he'd like a breath of sea air before driving back to London. I know you often go that way.'

'All right. I'll show him the way to the cliffs. I promise not to push him over. Not in term time anyway.'

Ewart Morgan was waiting outside. He had been making some notes on a small pad.

'I understand you'd like a breath of sea air before you return to muggy old London,' she said.

'We don't have fog any more,' he said, as if talking to a child. 'Smoke-less fuel, you know.'

Reah took the path through the shrubbery. It was a short cut to the cliffs and to the road which led to her flint-walled cottage in the small hamlet of Southdean, about a mile away.

The atmosphere was brittle. She could not think of a thing to say to this confident and successful man in his expensive London clothes. At the same time, there was nothing soft about him. He looked tough and ruthless.

They reached the Downs where the grass was rough and coarse; pale blue meadow crane's bills nodding fragile heads, yellow cowslips and ragwort growing among the gorse.

'This is National Trust land,' said Reah, breaking the silence.

In the distance were the verdant stretches of golf links and the estuary of the tidal river Cuckmere, flowing blue and peacefully between the fields to the sea. It was a view Reah loved. Below, the sea sparkled with dancing silver droplets.

'It's very beautiful,' he said. 'Well worth the wait.'

'I suppose you are used to having people at your beck and call; jumping to your every command,' she said.

'Something like that.'

'You could have found your own way.'

'I wanted you to show me.'

'I might have had better things to do.'

'What a firebrand you are,' he said, strolling over to the cliff edge. 'I suppose this is what comes from being a school teacher.'

'Your knowledge of the teaching profession is pretty naive,' said Reah, her hazel eyes flashing. 'The days of the dried up spinster with her hair in a bun went out with the Ark.'

'And more's the pity,' he said smoothly. 'I hardly think patched jeans and an old hat are any improvement. Quite the reverse. I can't see how your students can learn about being young ladies from your example.'

'Nor would they learn anything from your bad manners,' said Reah. 'Except, of course, they would learn what kind of man to avoid.'

They stopped walking and their eyes met in a cold, steely clash. Reah did not know why she should feel so threatened just by the very presence of the man. He was undeniably attractive. Reah turned away abruptly.

Along this small area of coast, the cliffs

were not high. They had not begun to tower as the sheer and awesome Beachy Head, nor the undulating Seven Sisters that rose on the far side of the estuary.

Reah had climbed these lower cliffs many times with her father. They held no fear. She turned her face into the wind and that was her undoing.

A sudden mischievous gust of sea breeze caught at the brim of her Trilby and tossed it first on the path, and then as she scrambled to catch it, tipped the hat over the edge of the cliff. Reah was more annoyed than alarmed.

She put down her bag and the book and peered over the edge. The hat was only a few feet down, but out of reach caught in some rough bush. It would be child's play to retrieve it.

'Surely you're not going to try and get it?'

'There's no way I'm going to lose my father's hat,' said Reah firmly.

'You're a fool.'

'I wouldn't expect you to stay and help. I hope you can find your way back to your car.' She waved vaguely in the direction he should take.

She eased herself over the top, slithering down a rain gully that gave sufficient grip for her feet, holding onto any sturdy root or jutting rock. She had to be quick. Any moment the errant wind might whip the hat into the air and spin it further down the face of the cliff into the surging sea.

But she reached it in time. She stuffed it inside her sweater, giving herself a unique third bust. Then she began the ascent.

Afterwards she could never work out why she got stuck, but somehow she took a different angle of direction and lost the helpful rain gully. She had not been concentrating.

It was maddening when she could see she was only a few feet from the top. One good heave and she would be perfectly safe. But there was nothing near enough to hold onto. There must have been a minor landslide after the last rain storm, for Reah did not recognise a single feature of the area above her. She moved cautiously sideways but found no easier way up. She was stuck on a small ledge only a few feet below the top.

She heard footsteps crunching along the path and it was the most welcome sound in the world.

'Hello there,' she called out. 'Can you help me? I'm down here. I can't move.'

The footsteps stopped and Reah looked up hopefully. She longed to see a burly farm labourer or a rugged hiker, all brawn and muscles.

The dark brown eyes of the playwright studied her with circumspection. She felt herself shrinking under his gaze.

'You do some rash things, don't you?' he said. 'I suppose you need rescuing.'

'Not exactly,' said Reah crisply. 'I could climb downwards, walk along the shore and then back inland along the estuary. But it would be much quicker and easier if you just gave me a hand up these last few feet.'

'Are you sure it's safe?' he asked, peering over.

'Of course it's safe,' said Reah. 'I've

climbed these cliffs a hundred times as a girl.'

'Why are you stuck then?'

'I don't know,' she said, exasperated. 'And I don't wish to have a lengthy discussion about the situation. I just want a helping hand to get off this ledge.'

'Helping hand on its way,' he said coolly.

He lay full length on the ground and stretched down his arms. It was all she needed. She grasped his hands to use him as a lever; suddenly surprised by the crushing strength of his grip on her. In moments she was scrambling up, Ewart transferring his hold to her armpit, then grabbing her waist and buttocks till he pulled her over the edge and onto the path beside him. It was very undignified. She lay on the rough ground, gasping.

She sat up, aware that Ewart was staring at her hair. The red mane was tumbled over her face, strands whipped across her eyes, caught in the lashes and stuck to the moisture on her lips. She fumbled under her sweater for her hat and crammed it down on her head, tucking her hair away furiously.

'You're laughing at me,' she accused.

'Don't be ridiculous,' he snapped, brushing bits of grass and dust off his immaculate safari suit. 'Aren't you in the least bit grateful that I heard your call?'

Reah drew a deep, shuddering breath. It went against the grain to thank Ewart Morgan for anything, but he had helped her and she had to say it.

'Thank you,' she said, almost inaudibly. 'I'm grateful for your help. It was very kind of you.'

'I am overwhelmed by the warmth of your thanks,' he said, his eyes passing over her, scant inches away. 'But I think I deserve something better.'

'I don't understand.'

'Of course, I forgot. Perhaps you are a little behind in the art of being a woman. The teaching profession is somewhat limited in that sphere.'

He leaned forward, pulling her to him. His mouth came down on her lips before she could object or struggle. It was a burning kiss, his mouth expertly seeking her softness, recklessly imprinting his masculinity on her slim body. She tried furiously to free herself from his arms. Suddenly he let her go and stood up. He was already striding back over the Downs before she had even regained her breath.

Reah put her trembling fingers to her bruised lips. She had never been kissed like that before. Her senses were shattered. Every nerve of her body was tingling. How dare he kiss her so intimately, invading the cave of her mouth. And yet something in her had almost leaped to meet his demand.

Taut and angry, Reah picked up her bag and parcel which she found further along the path, and turned towards home. She needed the familiarity of her cottage at Southdean to wrap round her like a high, protective wall.

She kept Miss Hardcastle's gift as a supper time treat.

It was a book, a big glossy coffee-table book of art. It was called simply

'Florence'. The pages fell open stiffly revealing the glory of the Renaissance city. Reah's coffee grew cold as she pored over photographs of the magnificent medieval churches, bell towers, palaces and museums. The preserved world of 14th and 15th-century culture beckoned like some beautiful Florentine enchantress. It was all there in the valley below the Tuscan hills, a small perfect city in total harmony with the span of time.

Reah's fingers twitched for a pencil, a pen. The great architecture drew her like a magnet.

TWO

Reah was apprehensive at the prospect of her holiday. She had been no further than Paris before, and that had been as a 15-year-old in the company of her father.

She sat on an upholstered sofa in the departure lounge at Gatwick, content just to be part of the throng of travellers. Memories of that stay in Paris came back, bringing pain and pleasure. Her father had been a wonderful companion, full of the joy of living.

'Everyone should see Paris in the Spring,' her father had said. It was in Paris that she had first thought about teaching art, to impart enthusiasm and knowledge to young people.

Reah checked her flight number to Pisa on the television monitors. The British Airways flight was still a long way down the list, slowly creeping up as each flight closed and took off.

'Miss Lawrence, isn't it?' a voice cut through the noise in the lounge. 'I never forget people I rescue. Not stuck on a cliff this morning?'

Ewart Morgan was looking down at her, not exactly pleased, as if he had almost walked by and then for no reason at all changed his mind.

'How amazingly observant you are,' said Reah sweetly. 'I had hoped never to see you again.'

'That hope was entirely mutual,' he said, sitting down beside her. He looked tired. She noticed faint shadows of fatigue deepening his eyes.

Everything about him was brown today. He wore coffee coloured slacks, a cinnamon brown jacket with gold buttons, toning silk shirt, no tie, both collars turned up as usual. His shoes were a shiny brown leather, very expensive, probably hand-made.

'Do you always price everybody's clothes?' he asked. 'It's a little disconcerting. I'll save my bills if you like.'

Reah coloured slightly. She could not help approving of his style, and there was no doubt about the aura of success that clung to the man. He was about thirty-five, young to have already gained such an international reputation. Even Reah, who was not a television addict, could name half a dozen of his plays.

'I've no interest in clothes,' said Reah coolly.

'That's obvious.'

The retort was not fair. Reah had made

an effort that morning with her limited wardrobe. Her jeans were well-cut; her crinkled dark peach blouson from French Connection; her slim feet in strappy bronze sandals. Her hair was looped back with two large tortoiseshell clips, and weeks of working in the garden of the cottage had given her skin the faintest tan. Several men had turned to look at her that morning and it was not just the colour of her hair which attracted their gaze.

Her BA flight to Pisa now had a gate number. Reah leaped to her feet, grabbing her bag, almost tripping over Ewart's outstretched legs.

'Leaving it a bit late, are you?' he commented, his eyes half closed. 'You'd better run. They might take off without you.'

She was pleased to find she had a window seat, fastened the clasp of the seat belt after stowing her bag by her feet, and waited for the plane to fill up.

She had never flown before but she was not going to tell anyone. Reah was not afraid, only apprehensive about a new experience.

'Excuse me, but you are sitting in my seat.'

Reah's spirits fell at the now recognisable voice. The accent was even more pronounced.

'I don't believe it,' she said blankly.

'You are in the right row, but the wrong seat,' said Ewart, glancing at the embarkation card still in her hand.

'Why are you here?'

'For the same reason as you—I want to get to Florence and this is the quickest way.'

So he was going to Florence, too. It was infuriating that Ewart Morgan should be going to the same city. He was the last person she wanted to see, anywhere.

'Don't worry,' he said casually. 'Although Florence is a small city, I doubt if we shall ever meet. My research will take me along different paths.'

'I am going to sketch buildings.'

'I'm more interested in people,' he said. His eyes were fixed on her face. 'I like to know what makes them tick, their motives for doing things, saying things. Buildings are just bricks and mortar.'

'Don't forget buildings are designed and built by people. They become an expression of themselves.'

'Ah...' He took off his jacket and put it in the overhead compartment. 'Thus speaks the dedicated art mistress.'

'I don't believe this is a coincidence at all,' said Reah with a spurt of indignation. 'I can't imagine why, but I think you actually arranged to take this flight and sit next to me.'

'The flight, yes. The seat, no...merely a computer fluke. I confess that I did know you were flying to Florence today. Miss Hardcastle told me. That nice lady has a soft spot for you. I happened to mention last week that I was going to Florence to research for a new play, and she asked me to keep an eye on you. She said you hadn't flown before, or been abroad on your own. How could I refuse? I almost felt sorry for you,' he added.

'There's no need to be sorry for me,'

said Reah, her colour rising slightly. 'I can manage perfectly well on my own.'

'That's a relief. I've really got far too much to do in the short time I shall be in Florence. But Miss Hardcastle is a gently persuasive lady. I began to feel quite saintly.'

'No need to feel like that on my behalf. I have everything arranged for my stay.'

'Then perhaps I could have my seat?'

Reah bent to shift her bag from the narrow space on the floor, forgetting that she had not unfastened the seat belt. Her fingers would not obey her as she struggled with the clasp; the fuselage doors clamped shut and the seat belt and no smoking signs went on. The big jet was ready for take-off.

'It's too late now,' said Ewart, fastening himself into the seat next to her. 'Stay where you are. I'm going to work.'

He took a folder out of his brief case and began to read through some papers.

Reah gripped the armrests as the Trident gathered speed along the runway. The vibration of the gigantic wheels shook her spine. The sense of speed was at the same time exhilarating and frightening.

Ewart noticed the clenched fingers and shot a glance at her tense face. At the very moment that the plane lifted off and went into a sharp angled climb, he put his hand over her own. She was acutely aware of his masculine presence. Trees and hedges were suddenly left below. The Surrey countryside became Lilliputian, the roads ribbons, fields a patchwork quilt of browns and greens.

Wisps of cloud streamed past the window, then there was nothing more to see as the plane climbed through a belt of thick cloud. It broke through into another world, dazzling with sunshine, the unbroken blue of the sky stretching endlessly.

Reah was spellbound. Ewart removed his hand without comment. They were soon over the English Channel and through breaks in the cloud she saw bobbing fishing boats and the sandy line of the French coast.

When she caught a first glimpse of the

majestic snow-crested Alps, she could not retain her excitement.

'Look, look,' she said, tugging Ewart's sleeve. 'The Alps! Aren't they beautiful?'

He leaned across her and she caught a whiff of his after-shave. It was a subtle, poignant scent and came as a surprise. Her father had smoked a pipe and the aroma of tobacco had always clung to him.

'Marvellous,' he agreed.

He was too close. There were strands of grey among the light brown hair falling over his ears. They were infinitely touching as if each grey hair was a sadness in his life, or the price of overwork. Her gaze wandered over his skin. He had a tiny blemish near the corner of his eye; a tiny mole that flawed his handsome features and made him vulnerable. His lashes were blunt and speckled, veiling his eyes now as he squinted against the bright sun.

She was trapped against the back of her seat. If he came any closer, she would not be able to resist touching his hair. It looked so fine, newly washed and she knew it would be soft. She imagined him standing in the shower as naked as Michelangelo's David, the soap suds running down his glistening brown skin.

Then Reah reminded herself who he was. This was no vulnerable, dreamy poet but a hard and ruthless writer.

It was unbearable. She shut her eyes with a sharp intake of breath.

'Ah, breakfast,' he said, bringing everything back to normal.

At Pisa airport, she lost him. They were queueing up to go through Immigration Control, and without a word he vanished. Reah told herself she did not want his company. After retrieving her suitcase, she found the coach going into the city.

It was hot. The Italian sunshine was much stronger than the English summer she had left behind.

Tuscany was a beautiful area; a region of thickly wooded hills, snowy peaks and lush vineyards laden with fruit. Rows of tall dark cypress trees marched up the hillsides, and the olive groves filled every space in the fertile valleys.

It was a long winding drive to the

outskirts of Florence. Even the outlying villages, picturesquely shabby, had their share of unexpected glory...an ancient church, a bell tower, a sprawling villa.

The city of Florence was a sun trap that lay within a circle of low hills. The dun-coloured river Arno, once a mountain torrent, flowed past little streets and under many bridges. Dominating the city was the immense terracotta dome, a feat of medieval engineering.

'Brunelleschi,' Reah murmured in awe.

Tourists thronged the pavements, gaping at every artistic achievement, while noisy little Fiats and Vespas ripped along the streets.

She had made a reservation through her local travel agent at an inexpensive pensione in a street some distance from the walled city centre. A bus dropped her off at the end of the small street and she was just congratulating herself on finding the pensione without any trouble, when she noticed something strange about the appearance of the narrow old house.

All the shutters were closed. She put

down her case and rapped the heavy brass knocker. There was no answer.

She wiped her damp hair back from her forehead. It was the hottest part of the day and she was longing for a wash and fresh clothes. She began to think that she ought to ask someone, but her Italian was minimal.

'Pensione Orsaira?' She stopped passers-by, waving her hands towards the shuttered house. They returned blank stares, then a neighbour appeared and in loud and rapid Italian explained the situation to Reah. She was no wiser.

'In English, please...' she pleaded, shaking her head.

A girl student came to Reah's aid. Her English was good enough to give Reah the bad news.

'The madre, the grand-madre, has died. The family go to funeral in Naples. Much family business to attend. Not return this week,' said the girl. 'You go Tourist Office in station.'

By the time Reah found the Tourist Office, her soft topped case seemed to weigh a ton. She was hot, sticky and worried about accommodation for the night.

The woman in the Tourist Office was helpful but not hopeful. Everywhere in Florence was fully booked. She could only offer the top luxury hotels or a crash pad at a youth hostel.

'A crash pad?' Reah felt she had reached the depths. She longed to give up the whole expedition and back track to her cottage in Southdean. The wonders of Florence no longer seemed worth the effort.

'The hostels are clean and cheap,' the woman re-assured her. 'You may have to share with two or three; some have dormitories. They are very popular and always full. You may only get one night. Shall I find a place for you?'

Reah nodded. She had no choice. The woman made some phone calls and then wrote down an address on a piece of paper with directions for finding the hostel. Reah thanked her, shattered by her bad luck. Perhaps some village would have rooms free. But she would not go without first seeing the giant cupola of Brunelleschi.

She had picked up a map in the Tourist Office. The Via de Panzani would lead her to the Piazza del Duomo, to the steps of the great cathedral, the Sante Maria del Fiore, the largest church in the world after St Peter's in Rome.

It was a tiring walk in the sunshine carrying her case. The red and green marble of the exterior of the cathedral was unexpectedly bright and took some getting used to. The great dome dwarfed everything in the busy, bustling square.

Next to the cathedral stood Giotto's 14th century Campanile, one of the most beautiful bell towers in the world. Reah had planned to climb its 414 steps to see the famous panoramic view of Florence's rooftops.

She was quite exhausted. She sank down onto a high, uneven curbstone, not bothered by the dozens of feet almost stepping on her; she was past caring.

A pair of expensive Ruchi brown leather shoes stopped a few feet away, hesitated, then returned. Reah did not look up. He

44

could laugh all he wanted to. She was too tired to move.

'What's the matter?' he asked sharply, looking closer at her pale face. 'Homesick already?'

Reah's hazel eyes filled with tears, but she blinked them back quickly.

She would not give him the satisfaction of knowing that her plans had gone awry and that after tonight, she had nowhere to sleep.

'Go away, please,' she moaned, hanging her head. The heat on the back of her neck was making her feel sick. She thought of her cool English garden, full of sweetpeas and marigolds, and she was ready to burst into tears.

'You'll get sunstroke sitting there,' he said brusquely, helping her to her feet. 'And get dehydrated. What have you had to drink? Nothing? I thought so. Come along, you stupid girl. You need some iced limone.'

Ewart picked up her case. Reah felt so ill she would have left it on the pavement. He took her arm and threaded through the pavement tables, and down a quieter side street. A little trattoria had a few tables outside shaded with green unbrellas.

'Have you eaten since our airline breakfast?'

Reah shook her head.

'For a school teacher, you have little common sense,' he said ordering a lasagne, lemonade and caffe freddo for himself. 'That's iced coffee,' he translated for her benefit.

Reah took a deep breath. Her strength was beginning to return. She brushed her hair away from her face, her forehead damp with the heat.

'I have had one hell of a morning,' she said. 'The last thing on my mind was food or drink. While you were settling into your air-conditioned luxury accommodation, I was tramping the streets in the sweltering heat trying to find somewhere to sleep tonight.'

'Didn't you make a reservation before you arrived? Florence is always packed out.'

'Of course I did; I am not that dim.

46

My travel agent booked me into a small pensione, but when I got there, it was completely shut up. The grandmother had died and the whole family has gone off to Naples for the funeral. I went to the Tourist Office in the station and they found me a crash pad for tonight.'

'Is that what I dread to think it is?'

'A youth hostel. Very basic.'

The signora arrived with a steaming plate of lasagne covered in a rich sauce, iced lemonade and iced coffee for Ewart.

'The signora makes the pasta herself. In the early morning you can see sheets of green pasta hung all over the chairs.'

Reah choked. 'Pasta hung chairs are a little hard to take especially when one is eating it,' she said.

She looked at the man who had tried to make money out of her father's death. She had imagined a monster; tough, Ewart Morgan might be but she also saw a very human person. He obviously did not connect her with the famous yachtsman. Nor did she want him to know.

'I'm here to write about the great flood,' he said with a wry grin. 'Disasters are my speciality.'

Reah knew only too well that disasters were his speciality, other people's tragedies. 'Oh you mean that flood,' she said. 'The one in 1966?'

His brown eyes darkened. 'It did an irrevocable amount of damage,' he said after a long pause. 'It destroyed thousands of priceless art treasures. The night of November 4. More than 200 millimetres of rain fell in twenty four hours. That's a quarter of the average annual rainfall for the whole of Italy. Four million cubic yards of water raced to the sea and broke the Arno's banks.'

Reah shivered despite the heat of the afternoon. She pushed away threads of her frightening dream; thrust away memories of her father's death. But she could not forget that it was this man, sitting opposite her, who was enmeshed in both haunting shadows. And here was water again, suffocating water...

'A great mass built up,' Ewart went on.

'Diesel oil, refuse, chemicals, dyes and tons of mud. A horrendous wave of slime hit Florence with fiendish force. It swept away houses, broke down doors, tossed cars in to piles, crushed monuments, uprooted trees, exploded furniture. It was a nightmare, Reah, not only for the thousands of people caught in the little streets and basements, but a disaster for the ancient treasures of Florence.'

'People were drowned?' she asked in a strained voice.

'Over forty. It was a miracle there were not many more. It was a public holiday and people were sleeping late in their beds. There was no panic or stampede to leave the city. People climbed higher and watched, stunned, as their beautiful city disappeared under water. Just imagine their feelings, Reah. When the water went, Florence was knee-high in stinking slime.'

'Why are you writing a play about it?'

'Where there's disaster, there's always courage. I want to write about the heroes and heroines. Prefetto, the Civil Governor. The bands of capelloni, the long-haired youths, who worked without pay and slept in unheated railway carriages. The rescue work is a tremendous story and I have forty-nine minutes in which to tell it.'

The Ewart Morgan she despised seemed to change in front of her. He obviously wrote from the heart once he was involved in his story. He might behave ruthlessly to get it, but there was a sensitivity softening his mouth now and in his eyes.

'You and I are in Florence for totally opposite reasons,' said Reah, brushing these thoughts aside.

Ewart nodded. 'You want to live in the past, nice and secure. I face the present. We are very different.'

It was true. Reah did live in the past, when she had been secure in her father's love and protection. The present was empty.

'What are you going to call your play?' she asked quickly.

He screwed up his eyes as if looking into the distance.

'I don't know what I'm going to call it. I use "Flood" as a working title, something to hang it on. I've no ideas... "Wall of Water" perhaps?'

'I must go,' said Reah, fumbling in the depths of her bag for some money. 'I must find this hostel before it gets too late. I'd like a wash.'

'You could have used the day hotel in the station,' he commented. 'Come along. I'll take you to the best wash and brush up joint in town.'

'No, thank you,' she said. 'I don't want to go anywhere with you.'

'Stop arguing. You're making a scene. People are looking at you.'

Ewart took her case and propelled Reah firmly towards the piazza. He began looking for a taxi to hail. Several yellow bodied taxies appeared immediately. He was that kind of man.

'Palazzo Excelsior,' he said, pushing Reah into the back of the taxi before she could protest again.

'Where are you taking me?' she demanded to know.

'Sit back and be quiet. One more ungrateful word and I'll tip you back onto the streets. Be a good girl and you can have a long cool bath, a civilised number of towels and a bathroom all to yourself. No sharing.'

The taxi swung round into the curved driveway of the Palazzo Excelsior. It was a beautiful old Florentine palace converted with skill and modernised into a deluxe hotel.

The old stone walls were a sun-warmed honey colour, the graceful arches giving shade to orange and lemon trees in large terracotta pots. Chestnut trees and vines grew in profusion; climbing roses climbed over everything. Wisteria bloomed on the walls like pale confetti.

Ahead she could see into the foyer, a cool spacious room with tall Venetian lamps, expensive antique furniture and acres of exquisite marbled floor.

'I can't go in there,' said Reah, conscious of the dust on the seat of her jeans, the sticky tangle of her hair, dirty hands, the crumpled blouson. 'I'll go to the day hotel in the station.'

'Don't be ridiculous,' said Ewart. 'I've

never met anyone so self-conscious.'

He took his key and ignored the polite, curious looks from the reception staff. 'Pretend you are a rich heiress in disguise. Act aloof and distant; tip the lift boy a few thousand lire. You've no idea how word will get around.'

Her lips curved in a quick smile. Ewart stopped and put his fingers lightly under her chin, tipping her face. He looked into her hazel eyes as if seeking something he had missed.

'Hey, that's better,' he said slowly. 'You can smile after all. Very nice, too. You should do it more often.'

They went up in the gilded lift to the second floor. The wide corridor was hushed and deeply carpeted. He put his key in a door and it swung silently open.

She went into a small foyer and then into the most elegant bedroom Reah had ever seen; it was all pale Florentine colours of cream and gold. The big bed was covered in a silken spread deeply edged with antique cream lace; the tall windows draped with matching silk curtains. Her feet sank into the deep pile of a cream carpet. More flowers stood on a low coffee table. An ice bucket stood on a silver tray with crystal glasses.

Ewart walked across the room to another door and pushed it open.

'All yours,' he announced.

The bathroom was palatial. He could have thrown a party in it. The decorator had forsaken his cream and gold colours of the bedroom and introduced pale blue for the bath and vanitory unit, with the same blue repeated in the lily patterned tiles on the wall. The cream carpet was laid in the bathroom and Reah glimpsed gold taps and a pile of fluffy towels folded on the side. She was tempted. A quick bath, then she would go.

She saw bath oil and bath crystals. Ewart touched a switch and soft music filled the room.

'Anything else you want?' he asked with mock servitude.

'A cup of tea,' Reah suggested mis-chievously.

She turned on the taps, tipped in a

generous amount of bath oil and slipped out of her clothes. As she slid under the water she surrendered herself to the bliss of its relaxing comfort. She dipped her head under, amazed that one minute she could be sitting on the pavement, lost in a big city, almost homeless, and the next having a bath in the most luxurious hotel in Florence.

The door to the bathroom opened and Reah gasped, swiftly covering her breasts with a big sponge. He was standing in the doorway, staring at her.

'Don't panic. I can't see anything interesting with all this steam. Besides you are hardly my type. I prefer a more feminine woman. I couldn't get any tea. Perhaps this will do instead.'

She heard the chink of something being stood on the wide edge of the bath and then the door closed. It was a tall tulip-shaped glass full of golden bubbles. She sniffed its delicate aroma, tasted the drink, her hand trembling. It could only be champagne. She took a few sips, trying to quell the jangling awareness of his gaze on her body. How dare he...if he came in again, she would throw something at him.

She made sure the door was properly closed and soaped herself thoroughly... champagne in the bath. He certainly had style.

When she eventually came out of the bathroom, cool, clean and a little drowsy, Ewart had gone. She trailed across to the windows, wrapped in yards of bath towel, and looked down on the piazza below. It was suffused with rosy afternoon sunlight; children playing with a ball, nuns walking in pairs, old men sitting on the pavement watching the world go by. She could smell rosemary and lavender from the enclosed garden below.

She yawned, wrapping the towel more firmly round her body. The big bed was soft and inviting. She turned back the cover and pulled over a plump linen-cased pillow. She would just close her eyes for five minutes.

She awoke when she felt a weight tip down the side of the bed. Sleepily she opened her eyes, then quickly retrieved the bath towel and pulled it up round her shoulders.

Ewart's eyes were dark and expressionless, roving over her bare skin, her young face glowing with sleep. The tumbled mane of hair was still damp, and there was nothing she could do to conceal the rise and fall of her small breasts beneath the towel.

The sheer arrogance of his nearness as he sat on the side of the bed made Reah frighteningly aware of his strength. He knew it too.

Reah felt her heart quicken. Instinctively she drew back, fighting down her panic-stricken thoughts. What a fool she was, to have let herself get into such a vulnerable position. Seduced by one glass of champagne.

'I offered you the use of my bath, not my bed.'

The voice was mocking. She expected any moment to be fighting him off but he did not move. She turned her head away, hiding her fear. Her pulse quickened.

She felt his mouth on the skin of her bare shoulder. It was a kiss as light as a butterfly's touch. She felt her body tremble, remembering that other kiss.

She was appalled by her own yearning weakness as that chaste kiss sent a warning quiver through her limbs. She struggled for composure, refusing to meet his speculative eyes.

Suddenly Ewart got up and walked over to the wall wardrobe. He began to pull out the hangers, piling shirts, slacks and jackets over his arm.

'What are you doing?' she asked.

'You can stay here,' he said. 'You can have my room. I'm moving into a suite at the back which has just become vacant.'

'No, thank you,' said Reah, sitting bolt upright, clutching the towel to her. 'I don't want your room.'

'I prefer the suite,' said Ewart, as if he had not heard a word of what she said. 'It's at the back and it'll be quieter. I'll be able to get more work done.'

'Thank you for the use of your bathroom,' said Reah, swinging her slim legs off the side of the bed. 'I'm going.'

'You're staying here,' he said, pulling open drawers and piling socks onto a chair. 'It's all been arranged.'

'Who asked you to interfere in my life?' Reah said, pulling the towel round her with as much dignity as she could muster. 'Who do you think you are? My guardian or something?'

'Stop fussing,' he said, his eyes glittering. 'Accept your good fortune. Most girls would give their eye teeth to stay at the Palazzo Excelsior.'

'Well, not me,' Reah snapped. 'It's a ridiculous idea. For a start, I could never afford it. This place must cost a fortune.'

'If you want to,' he said, a sardonic gleam in his granite eyes. 'You could repay me in kind,' he added.

'No thank you,' said Reah, outraged. 'Never, and I mean absolutely never. I'm going.'

'I'm afraid I must overrule you for your own sake. It would be very foolish to start wandering about Florence now looking for this hostel. It'll be dark soon. As to repaying me...amusing how Englishwomen always jump to one conclusion. I said nothing about rape or seduction. I merely meant that you might sew on a few buttons, run a few errands...and I might think of something else.'

'For all this...you're joking?' Reah waved her arm to encompass the luxurious room, then clutched at the slipping towel. She edged towards the bathroom. She would feel happier with her clothes on.

'I really can't understand why you are making such a fuss. Anyone would think I was carting you off to Siberia, instead of seeing that you have a civilised roof over your head for the night.'

'Funny you should say that...the atmosphere is pure Siberia. I can't think when I've ever been in a situation I've liked less. You're constantly interfering, and I can manage very well without you.'

Ewart shot her an impatient glance. 'I've noticed how well you manage. I insist that you stay.'

'Then I insist that I pay for myself.'

He shrugged his shoulders. 'As you will.

I'll waste no more time arguing with you. Get some clothes on and I'll see you in the bar in half an hour.'

Reah sat on the edge of the bed and gazed in disbelief at these luxurious surroundings in the heart of a medieval Florentine palace. She ran her hand lightly over the silken cover; it was very beautiful.

There was a rap on the door. She knew Ewart would not knock.

Reah put on a thin cotton robe. She peered round the door. It was a uniformed page boy carrying a large flat white box tied with striped red ribbon.

'Signora Lawrence?'

'For me? I haven't ordered anything.'

'It is delivered by order of Signore Morgan.'

'I see. Grazie.'

The box was from a famous Roman fashion house. Reah felt a small spurt of anger. Anger that Ewart Morgan dared to think that she had nothing suitable to wear at the Palazzo Excelsior; that he had the impudence to buy clothes for her; that he should tempt her by buying from one of the most exclusive Roman designers.

She untied the ribbon and lifting off the lid, removed swathes of tissue paper from round the dress.

She caught her breath and held it up. Her heart fell. She had to admit he had the most perfect taste.

It was a soft silk chiffon dress, silvery mink in colour, a straight and simple dress falling in tiny pleats from narrow shoulders. It looked like a shaft of moonlight warmed by the glow of candles. The subtle colouring and the pure simplicity of the design appealed to Reah most strongly. She could not resist trying it on.

She put on a lacy bra and brief pants and slipped the dress over her head. It was sheer magic. She would never have chosen such a strange colour, but the contrast with her red hair and lightly tanned skin was unbelievable. She slipped her feet into strappy sandals.

Reah rarely wore make-up but she knew

the dress demanded that nature should be dramatically enhanced. With an artist's skill she brushed smoky shadow round her hazel eyes, lengthened her lashes with mascara, highlighted her fine cheek bones with blusher and finally outlined her lips with the softest of rose lipsticks.

Then she took her mane of hair and twisted it onto the top of her head, securing it with pins and tortoiseshell clips. Damp tendrils curled round her cheeks and neck like an Edwardian beauty.

She took a long look at herself in the full length mirror, wishing she had a single piece of jewellery or some French perfume. She hardly recognised the slim and beautiful woman who stood there, the shimmering dress clinging to her body, her radiant hair like a shining crown.

'Yes. You'll do. Come along. I've been waiting ten minutes already.'

Ewart was leaning against the doorway. He had changed into a dark blue velvet jacket, light slacks, a Givenchy shirt finely tucked and open at his tanned neck.

'I'm not wearing it,' said Reah.

'Unless my eyes deceive me, you are wearing it,' he said, barely concealing his amusement.

Reah wished he had not caught her trying it on. She should have returned the box to him straight away, unopened.

'I intend to change,' said Reah with some dignity.

'Later. I booked a table in the restaurant and we are already late.'

'I—'

'Are you ever going to stop arguing with me? It would be pleasant if we could manage to have a meal together without this constant disagreement.'

'I don't want the dress.'

He sighed with exasperation. 'I'll put it on the bill. Will that satisfy you? At least you look more like a woman now.'

Reah fought down an angry retort.

'What are we waiting for?' she said. 'A civilised meal sounds nice.'

She spoke huskily, suddenly all woman. Despite what she knew of Ewart Morgan, she was drawn to him. It was a heady feeling.

THREE

Reah was out before breakfast while the leaves still hung with dew and the air of Florence was drenched with sweetness.

She had a sketch pad, pens and pencils in a bag slung over her shoulder.

She had resolved before arriving in Florence that she would not attempt to draw the whole of a great building or statue. It had already been done many times by people far more talented than herself.

She would instead take a particular aspect of a sculpture—a foot, a hand, the angle of an elbow—and of a building some architectural detail, an oculus, a pulvin, a cornice or a span of stone arch that defied gravity.

Her feet took her first to the little streets where, since medieval times, each one specialised in a trade—the street of silks, the street of shoes, the street of caged birds where ravens, robins, canaries and nightingales filled the early morning air with their plaintive song. In another street the shopkeepers were putting out fruit, mushrooms and ripe cheeses from every region of Italy, the produce cradled in leaves of oak and chestnut and vine. The aroma of coffee from the rough sacks propped against each other reminded Reah that she had not had breakfast.

Supper with Ewart had been an oasis of order in a chaotic day. He guided her through the menu, talking pleasantries. The meal had been delicious...veal escalope cooked in cream and wine, then Ewart recommended the torta della nonna—a light cream flan with almonds.

They took their coffee onto the garden terrace, the night air enfolding them into intimacy, still full of the day's heat but without its stifling oppression.

Reah, still feeling a different person in her shimmering dress, found herself drawn to Ewart against her will. His face was thrown starkly into a gauntness under the shadows of the overhead vine and his eyes glittered. He had the look of a medieval knight lean from war and famine but with the fierce strength of his heritage. There was a remoteness about him that was unfathomable.

'Miss Hardcastle will be pleased,' said Reah, accepting a second cup of coffee from the waiter.

'I beg you pardon?'

'The way you are keeping an eye on me. You'll be able to report back that you rescued me from the streets, put a roof over my head, fed me, even put a suitable dress on my back. Not bad for one day's work. Miss Hardcastle should be impressed.'

'Do I detect a note of scorn? I take it you are not similarly impressed, or in the slightest way grateful,' he said with infuriating accuracy.

Reah took a deep breath and hardened her resolve. She was aware that he had delivered her from a possibly uncomfortable experience in a dormitory in a crowded hostel. Delivered was an apt word. She was beginning to feel like a parcel.

'I am grateful,' she said, lowering her eyes. 'I appreciate that the Palazzo Excelsior is a far cry from a bed for one night in an unknown youth hostel on the outskirts of Florence, but I do object to the high-handed way you arranged it. You didn't even bother to ask me what I thought.'

'Would you have agreed to staying here if I had asked you? Of course not, you would have gone charging off to your crash pad, full of indignation and probably got lost on the way. The only way of dealing with you is to go ahead, and tell you afterwards.'

'Thank you for the warning,' she said crisply. 'Now I know what to expect. I'll remove myself from the Palazzo Excelsior as soon as I can find alternative accommodation.'

'Please yourself,' he said, draining his coffee.

He stood up. 'I've got notes to go over for tomorrow. A day is wasted if I don't write something.'

'I understand. But there are times when it's impossible to work. If there's a complete block.'

'An emotional block?'

Reah nodded, hating the huskiness in her voice. 'An artist gets an emotional block as if part of you had died and withered away. It's impossible to be creative. Perhaps it's different for writers.'

She had lost all inspiration to paint since her father's death; part of her had drowned with him in the sea. Anguish slashed across her heart as she thought of her father. Stanford Lawrence, tall, bearded, with a great deep laugh and big strong hands that had nursed her so gently through childhood illnesses. She shut her eyes tightly against the memories.

'There's no easy way,' she heard Ewart saying. 'The only answer is to pick up a pen and work.'

As Reah roamed Florence that morning, that lost feeling stirred within her. Her fingers were longing to hold a pencil, to feel smooth paper beneath the palm of her hand, to have the lightning message between eye and brain move down her arm and translate itself onto paper.

There was so much to see. Reah wandered through alleyways, courtyards, cloisters, not wanting to miss any glory or splendour. She began to feel dizzy with so much to take in; her pad started to fill with little sketches.

She came into the Piazzale degli Uffizi, outside the famous Uffizi Gallery, and found herself ankle deep in broken flowers and leaves. The early flower market was over and the stall holders were sweeping up the debris. The scent of fresh flowers was heavenly.

She bent and picked up a yellow rose, its stem crushed but the bud still perfect. She marvelled at the curves of its fragile velvet petals. The stall holder paused to lean on his broom and threw her a kiss.

'Grazie,' she smiled, and that seemed payment enough for the man, for he put his hand on his heart and sighed dramatically.

'I said you should smile more often.

You've made his day, and no, I am not following you.'

Ewart was regarding her mockingly with a glimmer of amusement. He was wearing a cool pilot-style shirt, open necked of course, and belted dark jeans. She was momentarily disconcerted when he turned to look at her sketch pad and his arm brushed against her.

There were soft dark hairs on his arm growing almost down to his wrist; the open buttons of his shirt revealed the beginning of hair on his chest, not swarthy but brown and virile. Reah knew, with a tightening of her nerves that it would be as fine and soft as a baby's hair to touch.

'You are always turning up,' said Reah.

'I have an elusive nature,' he said solemnly. 'I like creating surprises. These are quite good,' he added indicating her sketches.

'You don't have to patronise me,' she said, snatching them away. 'They're not finished.'

'Surely you know by now that I never say anything I don't mean. If I say your sketches are quite good, then accept my opinion without getting touchy.'

'Sorry,' said Reah. 'Yes, I am touchy about my work, especially before it's finished. If anyone says something too soon, the feeling can go and the picture is spoilt.'

He nodded. 'It can happen with my work.'

He looked at the yellow rose bud in her hand and then at her outfit.

'I presume the gear is a Miss Hardcastle special,' he said, lazily admiring her long bare legs.

Reah had not know what to wear that morning. The luxury of the palazzo was a little overpowering. She decided that reverse thinking would be her salvation. She had taken scissors to her second-best jeans and chopped the legs off above the knee. She had tied the ends of a faded, well-washed blue shirt high under her breasts, leaving a cool bare midriff. She was determined to beat the heat today. The result was stunning; the pale blue against her hair, her slim figure so feminine and enticing.

His eyes ran over her with a disturbing intimacy.

But she was unconscious of her allure. She did not see herself as a beauty; she saw only her flaws.

'Oh yes,' she said flippantly. 'I wear this at prize-givings. Can I buy you a coffee? I noticed a pretty little cafe facing the river.'

'Okay, thanks,' he said after the briefest pause. It was a long time since anyone had bought him anything. Because he was successful and rich from his success, it always seemed expected that he would pay. Now this long-legged, red-haired girl in shorn jeans was treating him to coffee, demonstrating their equality. He liked it. 'Lead on.'

They sat with big steaming cups of frothy coffee and freshly baked rolls. The riverside cafe was quiet, the tables still damp from scrubbing, the air clean and invigorating. They sat watching people on their way to work. There were few tourists about.

She found herself watching his face closely. That inner camera was working again. The lines of strength in his jaw would endure, eyes become darker, hair greyer...he would grow more and more attractive with the years.

He did not offer to pay. He rose, thanked her and said he had to go and see a man about a hero.

'Remember to stop and drink,' he warned. 'Don't get dehydrated. Just to make sure, I'll meet you at the "Perché no?" at noon and treat you to the best ice cream in Florence.'

'All right,' said Reah, trying to sound off-hand. They were parting, going their separate ways, free spirits, individuals, and yet...something indefinable existed even if it was only conflict; a strange, exhilarating feeling.

After a morning crammed with sight-seeing, she discovered Florence's ice cream mecca in Via dei Ravolini. Her mind was staggering under the richness of treasures in every street, at every corner.

'Would you like an ice cream?' he asked,

appearing out of the crowd. The stifling heat, noise and crowds had ruffled his hair and his shirt was damp with perspiration.

'Why not?' she murmured.

He chuckled and she wondered what was funny. He nodded towards the name of the shop. 'Perché no means why not. Come inside and choose your flavour.'

The choice was bewildering. Oxborough offered little more than vanilla, strawberry and chocolate. It had been a great day when mint arrived. She took so long deciding that Ewart became impatient and ordered a triple sundae. It arrived—three scoops of mocca, orange and almond, topped with whipped cream. It was his favourite.

'Quite delicious,' said Reah, savouring the taste of each flavour. 'I hereby resolve to try three different flavours every day and who cares about becoming fat.'

Reah had momentarily forgotten that she had sworn to hate the name Ewart Morgan for the rest of her life. The magic of Florence had her in its grip, binding her with invisible threads.

It was surprising that he did not seem to connect her with Stanford. 'I've been to the Tourist Office in the station and they are making enquiries for me. I'm sure they'll find me somewhere.'

'I think you're being very foolish. Why don't you simply stay at the Excelsior? It would save a lot of time and trouble.'

'Because I don't wish to,' said Reah defiantly. 'Firstly I can't really afford to squander money recklessly on such an expensive place. We are not all over-paid for our talents.'

'And secondly?' he enquired with a slight lift of his brows, ignoring the jibe at the financial success of his plays.

'Secondly I have no intention of remaining in the same hotel as you. I came to Florence to enjoy myself, and being organised by you is not my idea of enjoyment.'

'Nor mine, incidentally. At least we agree on that point. I've wasted enough time.'

'You need not waste a minute more. I can manage perfectly well now.'

His hand slipped round her waist in an insolent manner. Reah flinched. She could feel his fingers prodding her bare skin.

'There's room for a bit of flab,' he suggested flippantly. 'You're far too skinny.'

Reah removed his hand firmly.

'Funny how men think they can put their hands on a woman as if they have a right,' she said. 'I wouldn't dream of touching you in such a familiar way.'

'Why not?' he asked. She knew he was mocking her. It was infuriating. 'I might even like it, but then I probably wouldn't...you are hardly a sophisticated woman and the experience might be rather tame.'

If the cafe had not been crowded and the ice cream too good to waste, Reah would have been tempted to tip the lot in his face.

'Then again, it might not,' she retorted. 'Fortunately you are never likely to find out.'

Ewart stood up. 'If you are still around, I'll see you at supper,' he said. It was more of a command than a casual word of parting.

The Tourist Office was closed. It was the hottest part of the day and Reah's shorn jeans were clinging to her legs. With a heavy heart she went back to the hotel, realising that she dare not check out without an alternative reservation. She changed into a simple cotton skirt and blouse, and sponged her face. For all her brave words, she was worried.

The streets of Florence were stifling, but Reah made herself go out again. She was going to be first in the queue outside the Tourist Office when it opened. She was dismayed to find a scattering of people already waiting.

'But we made a reservation for you last night, Miss Lawrence, and you did not turn up,' said the woman behind the counter when it was Reah's turn.

'Yes, I know. I'm sorry,' said Reah. 'I met an acquaintance...someone from England. I was given a room at—er—this person's hotel.'

It sounded so unconvincing and illicit

that Reah found herself colouring.

'You were very lucky to get a room. Can't you continue at your friend's hotel?'

'But he's not a friend and I've no wish to stay there,' Reah went on, determined to correct the implied situation but somehow making it sound worse. 'I want to stay somewhere else.'

'I'm afraid that may not be possible,' said the woman, obviously feeling less helpful than yesterday. 'A lot of people would have been grateful for that bed last night.'

'I've said I'm sorry.'

'I've nothing to offer you if you don't like hostel accommodation.'

'I didn't say that...'

'Come back tomorrow. We may have something suitable for you then.'

'Grazie.'

Reah made her voice sound humble, but her feelings were outraged. It was Ewart's fault. If he had not been so high-handed, she would be on her way to some little pensione by now.

She realised she would have to stay at

the Palazzo Excelsior now. But that did not mean she need see Ewart, though he seemed to think she would be having supper with him.

Reah had no intention of doing any such thing. She would stand him up. It would be a small gesture of defiance at the way he simply took it for granted that she would be there.

She would appear...looking absolutely ravishing, them calmly tell him that she had made other plans for the evening.

Reah realised that if she was going to appear looking marvellous then she would have to buy something to wear. She had no intention of wearing the silvery silk chiffon dress again. She would have to get another stunning dress.

The dress shops of Florence were superb and very expensive. She would be digging deep into her savings again.

Reah had a fascinating hour wandering round the fashion boutiques. She was looking for something special but low key. When she found it, she knew instantly she need look no further.

It was a simple dress in eau de nil silk, full skirted with a tiny tie belt, the scooped neck edged with plaited material. It was the long sleeves that drew Reah's justification for the price. They were slashed dramatically so that her bare arms showed with every movement.

It fitted perfectly. The astute shop assistant hurried away and returned with a pair of ankle strap sandals in soft pale green leather. Reah could not resist them. She paid without a qualm.

She spent what was left of the afternoon sketching the frescos in the great Duomo Cathedral which she could appreciate now she was more refreshed. She began to plan a course for her pupils on Florentine art. She returned to the Palazzo Excelsior looking forward to a leisurely bath and dressing for dinner.

She soaked in the warm scented bath water wishing she had a glass of champagne to complete the decadent feeling. She washed her hair and brushed it till it shone like fire. Her make-up was applied with the subtle, steady hand of an artist.

The pale eau de nil silk dress draped softly over her slender figure, the colour a perfect foil for the highlights in her bright hair.

Her heart was racing as she went downstairs. He might make one of his sarcastic remarks but it would not matter. No man could fail to see that she could look like a woman if she wanted to...that was all she wanted to prove.

Reah hesitated at the entrance to the bar. She was not used to going into a bar alone. Ewart was already there, immaculate in a light-weight grey suit, very Italian, cream silk shirt open-necked, the collar casually turned up.

He came over with a glass of wine which he handed to her. She smiled cool thanks. Now she would tell him she had a date.

'I have to go out,' he said immediately. 'You'll have to eat on your own.'

'Oh,' Reah was stunned. The announcement was so unexpected. 'Do you have to see another man about a hero?'

'No, this time it's a lady. The Contessa Bianca Bernini. I thought it would be more polite if I took her to dinner.'

'Yes, of course,' said Reah, her face stiff with disappointment and annoyance that she had not made her announcement first.

'Will you be all right?'

'I'm used to looking after myself. Anyway I had already made other arrangements for the evening. I've got a date.'

There was a bitter tone to her voice. Ewart noticed but did not comment. He did not want to be late. He had been all day tracking down the elusive Contessa and it was a fifteen minute drive to her villa outside Florence. His work came first.

He left her holding the compensatory glass of wine. She drank it in one minute as it it were water. She dare not order another in case she did not have enough lire to pay for it. It would be better if she ate out at a cheaper trattoria.

She found a small place nearby, clean and unpretentious and ordered cannelloni from the chalked menu board. But she kept imagining Ewart wining and dining the Contessa and her appetite fled. She sat in the gathering twilight watching the couples strolling, arms entwined, and she felt very alone.

There had never been a special young man in her life because there had always been her father. A few boy-friends had come and gone while she was at Art College, but she had never fallen in love.

The only man she had loved was her father. Even now she could not believe that her father had died. How could someone be sharing breakfast with her one moment, and then a few hours later he had gone...forever.

Reah pushed away the plate. She would go back to the hotel and put colour washes on some of the ink drawings she had made that day.

She hurried upstairs to her room and took off the pale silk dress. Ewart had not even noticed it. She wrapped her cotton robe round her, took out her paints and was soon absorbed.

When her eyes began to tire with the close work, she knew it was time to stop before she made mistakes. She rolled onto the bed, rubbing her eyes and yawning. She longed to sleep but the traffic was so noisy...perhaps it was a feast day or a holiday.

Had Ewart come back yet from his date with the Contessa? She sighed. It was none of her business.

The night was humid and close. The Tuscan hills seemed to be suffocating the city. Reah longed for a drink but did not dare drink the water from the tap. There was room service but did it function at this hour?

It was 1 a.m. Surely some little bar would still be open. She would buy a drink then walk until she was tired and ready for sleep.

Not thinking she put on the eau de nil dress and took a purse in her hand. The night porter nodded to her as she went out through the entrance.

The streets were cooler now with movement in the air. Many of the bars and little trattorias were already shuttered and closed, but Reah did persuade a woman to serve some limonata before locking the doors. She strolled into an unfamiliar area of Florence near the river. There were still people about.

Her new sandals were no longer quite so comfortable. If she walked much further she would develop a blister. Insects buzzed round the street lamps in swarms. Reah suddenly did not like being out by herself anymore.

She turned to re-track, fairly confident that she could find her way back to the hotel. The great dome of the Duomo was a landmark, and she knew she had only to keep this dark mass to her left and she would not get lost.

Two youths turned the corner and were facing her. They wore grubby jeans and tee shirts with slogans and badges; they were an untidy pair with unkempt black hair.

As Reah went to pass them, they blocked her way. Their eyes glittered in the darkness. She thought she caught a whiff of beer.

A tremor of fear swept through her. The youths jostled against her, their voices loud and jeering. She could not understand what they were saying.

'Excuse me,' she said boldly. 'I wish to pass.'

They caught her arms, one on either side, and began to turn her round, not gently but roughly.

Reah tried to struggle out of their grip, which seemed to delight them. They were like boys tormenting a captured animal.

'Let me go,' she cried. 'Let me go!'

Instinctively she aimed her high heels at their shins but it only brought a dangerous gleam into their narrowed eyes.

'Here take my money,' she said angrily, offering her purse.

They looked at each other and laughed. It was not her money they wanted though they might take that as well.

She froze, her breath locked in her throat, too scared to move. She was aware of footsteps hurrying, then running. A lean shadowy figure appeared in an archway. Suddenly the youths were torn away from their grasp on her arms, and a man was pushing them against the wall. Reah almost fell as she was released.

'Young hooligans! Clear off before I thrash you,' the man rasped. 'The lady does not care for your attentions.'

Reah stumbled backwards, gasping for breath. It was a Welsh knight. It was Ewart.

FOUR

He had the two youths pinned against the wall. They began blustering, but they were uncertain. They eyed his muscular frame, and he had the advantage of being in a towering rage. He did not look like a man to be trifled with too far.

'Cowards! Frightening a young woman on her own. You ought to be thrashed,' he threatened. He looked violent enough to carry out his threat, and the two youths exchanged glances. They began to back off, defiantly jeering but with less conviction. Their faces slackened, eyes darting for escape.

Suddenly twisting out of Ewart's grasp, they took to their heels and ran down the street, shouting over their shoulders.

Reah put out a hand to steady herself, fighting off a feeling of weakness.

'Are you all right?' His voice was harsh and deep.

She nodded numbly.

'Did they hurt you?'

'No...'

She found herself being held close to his hard chest. His hand was in her hair, stroking her with amazing tenderness; then abruptly he pushed her away, shaking her like a naughty child.

'You little fool,' he exploded. 'What are you doing out here at this time of night, in this area, on your own? Haven't you any sense?'

Reah could not stop shivering despite the warmth of the night.

'I despair of you,' he said, tipping her head back so that she had to look at him. She was willing herself not to cry in front of him. 'Don't you know that a young woman walking alone at night in Italy is asking for trouble?'

She shook her head despairingly, strands of hair masking the tears on her cheeks. 'I never thought...please, Ewart, don't be so angry. I can't stand any more...'

'Italian men, especially young students, think that such conduct is an open invitation. And look at your dress. For heaven's sake, you were just asking to be accosted.'

'My dress?' A spark of indignation rose through her fright. Now he was being unfair. 'What's wrong with my dress? It's perfectly respectable. You couldn't have anything more modest.'

His face was forbidding in the darkness. Had he held her gently, or had she dreamed it? It could not be the same man.

'Those slashed sleeves. Don't you know how sexy that tantalising glimpse of female flesh is to men? Especially Italian men. It's a wonder you weren't accosted half a dozen times.'

Reah crossed her arms to cover the offending slits. Her fingers went inside the sleeves, to the smooth skin.

'I could walk around Southdean perfectly safely in this dress,' she said obstinately. 'I can't believe Italian men are so easily turned on.'

'My dear Reah...' Ewart steered her out of the dimly lit street. 'You don't seem to know how much your colouring attracts Italian men—that red hair and pale peachy skin.'

He draped his jacket over her shoulders. It radiated warmth from his body. She held it against her, the faint tang of his after-shave still clinging to it.

'What were you doing here in the Pinzochere...the grey area? This is not the most salubrious district.'

'I didn't know. I only came out for a walk. I couldn't sleep and I wanted a drink...it was so hot and noisy,' she tried to explain.

'It is warm and noisy,' his anger evaporating as he saw the tears still in her wide frightened eyes. 'It's far too beautiful a night to sleep.'

'Is the Contessa beautiful?'

'Very.'

'And you took her out?'

'No. We ate at her villa. There was a meal prepared. It was very civilised.' He stressed the last word fractionally.

'Is is a modern villa? With a large estate?' Reah was talking for talking's sake, hugging his jacket round her.

'No...they have a beautiful old villa, so mellow it almost merges into the hills. It's been in the family for years. They are wealthy and very aristocratic.'

'How did you happen to come along, just then?'

'I was out walking,' he said enigmatically.

'Keeping an eye on me, you mean,' said Reah stiffly.

'If you care to put it that way. But it was just as well I came along. Those two thugs were an ugly pair. You didn't stand a chance. Why on earth did you go out?'

'I was thirsty.'

'Heavens, child. I wasn't aware that there was a drought at the hotel. Haven't you heard of room service?'

'Don't call me child,' said Reah, worn out. 'Why are you so critical? Do you think you're perfect?'

'No, I'm not. But I shall call you child until you stop behaving like one.'

Reah made a conscious effort to calm down.

A new sound came clip-clopping along the street. It was one of the horse carriages which took tourists on sight-seeing trips round the city. Ewart grabbed her hand and hurried towards the sound of the hooves.

Ewart hailed the driver, but the old man shook his head and tapped his watch. Ewart took out a wad of lire notes, making the driver an offer he could not refuse. The sturdy grey and white dappled horse pawed the ground.

Ewart helped Reah climb up the swaying step.

'I think a leisurely drive through the park will be refreshing and peaceful. Then he'll take us back to the hotel. I will pay him enough to take tomorrow off, so he's happy.'

'Perhaps the horse is tired too,' said Reah.

'I should have known you were a softie. I forgot to ask the horse.'

The horse seemed to know where it was going without any guidance from the driver who was nodding on his perch. It turned into the Cascine, the beautiful public park that stretched along the right bank of the Arno. The site had once been the hunting ground and farms owned by the Medici family, and there was still a strong rural atmosphere.

It was a solitary place at night. The riders had gone home, and the shady paths were empty. Silvery leaves dipped and rustled as the carriage rolled by.

Ewart's arm slipped easily round her shoulder, drawing her close to his side. Reah felt herself stiffen, her natural reaction to any advance.

'Stop worrying, Reah darling,' he said unexpectedly. 'You are safe with me. I'm much too old for any undignified wrestling in the back of a carriage. I prefer a king-sized bed with taped music, or the bank of a mountain stream,' he added half to himself. His voice sounded far away.

'A mountain stream?'

'Imagine an Alpine meadow, high in the mountains. No one about for miles and the air clear and sweet. Sun glistening on snow tops, and further down the mountain a soft bank of meadow flowers for a bed. The only sound is the music from the little stream. What could be a more perfect setting for the act of love?' His expression was unfathomable, unapproachable.

She wanted to ask him if he had been to such a meadow with a woman he loved but she dared not. There must have been many women in his life.

'No,' he went on, answering her unspoken question. 'I've not yet found the right woman to take there. She will have to be very special to share my dream.'

Reah felt an awareness growing; she did not want to feel like that about any man, especially not Ewart.

She noted that he had not asked her about her evening and she was glad. She did not want to have to invent a gallant escort. She did not lie convincingly. Even as a little girl, her father had always known. The tiniest white lie had never escaped being rumbled by a great burst of laughter from him.

Ewart felt her shiver and his arm tightened. He did not know that she was thinking of her other dream, her nightmare.

'Tell me, teacher. Do you know the kind of woman I am looking for? What will she be like? Will she be stubborn, head-strong, with red hair and a lost, lost look in her hazel eyes?'

Her pulses quickened...a strange sensation tingled through her veins.

'Of course not,' said Reah, trying to sound normal. 'Quite the reverse. I should have thought a tall, elegant blonde would be more your style.'

'You're absolutely right,' he agreed amiably. 'I shall remember that...a tall, elegant blonde. Excellent advice.'

The swaying carriage was taking them deeper into the magical woods; the breeze playing with her hair till it shone with red lights and tawny shadows. The fine bones of her face were sharpened by the moonlight.

'The next best thing to an Alpine meadow,' he murmured unexpectedly.

She did not know when he began kissing her. They were tiny, tentative kisses at first, tasting the softness of her still lips, telling her not to be afraid...little kisses hovering over her pale eyelids, touching her brow, her cheeks. She moved her head in wonder, not knowing before that a man could be so gentle and patient.

This could not be Ewart Morgan; it must be some other man who looked like him. She felt herself melting into a slow trance...

His lips kissed a path down her cheek, round the curve of her ears and then buried themselves into the softness of her neck. His hands lifted her hair and as she obediently bent her head forward, soft whispering kisses found the roots of her hair at the back of her neck. The touch was exquisite, sending tingles of delight along her spine.

She responded with a growing warmth that surprised and astonished her. His mouth began to demand the sweetness inside her lips, and with a little moan she returned his passion, her arms creeping round his neck and entwining themselves in to an embrace.

His hands sought the softness of her arms through the slashed sleeves and his light stroking was a foretaste of the pleasure he could give to a woman. Reah felt her senses reeling away into the dizzy night; letting herself drift on waves of pleasure.

'Palazzo Excelsior,' said the driver gruffly. He noticed the young woman's tousled hair and glowing cheeks and thought sadly of his lost youth. There was only the television left for him now. Nights of kissing were over.

'Buona notte a grazie,' said Ewart, helping Reah down the step.

The driver nodded, pocketing the generous tip. 'Grazie. Buona notte, signore.'

The lights of the hotel seemed over bright, as Reah followed Ewart, walking in some hazy dream.

'I expect I look as if I've been thoroughly kissed,' she said a little nervously.

He caught her hand, 'Don't be ashamed of being beautiful and desirable.'

Ewart escorted her to her room and opened it with the key. He leaned on the wall, slim and taut, his dark eyes lazy and half smiling.

'I think I've chased away that frightened look,' he said taking her in his arms again, cradling her against his chest, kissing the top of her head.

'Frightened look?'

'Sometimes I see you looking at me as if you are afraid. There's a deep fear somewhere in your eyes. Tell me why.'

Reah shivered despite the warmth of the night.

'What are you thinking?' He was so sensitive to her emotions. 'When I spoke of my dream, you shivered.'

'I, too, have a dream,' she said in a voice so low he had to bend to hear it. 'But it's not like your dream of meadows and streams. Mine is awful. Mine is a nightmare. Mine is about deep water and waves and a drowning.'

Her voice fell away.

'And am I in your dream?' he asked.

'Yes. You are there.'

'Tell me about it,' he said. It was a command. He was making her put the horror into words. There was a sudden constriction in her throat.

The night air was still warm; outside a rare nightingale sang in competition with the noisy scooters. Through the window Reah could see a thousand leaping fireflies in the garden.

'I must get some sleep,' she said. 'I'm not used to staying up half the night. I shall be a wreck tomorrow.'

'It is tomorrow,' said Ewart. 'It's almost to-day. Soon you'll hear the church bells. In the middle of the day, when it's very hot, you should take a siesta instead of chasing round Florence. It's a civilised way of living.'

'Not in Southdean,' said Reah.

'How very neatly you have completely changed the subject. It's a disconcerting habit, Reah, but it doesn't work on me.

I'm not one of your nubile pupils who can be easily diverted. We were talking about your dream, your nightmare. Or would you rather that I kissed you again?'

Ewart's calm, almost arrogant assumption that she would like to have him continue kissing her cut through the tentative closeness that she had begun to feel. She reminded herself fiercely of his earlier relentless hounding with contempt; she had been seduced by the romantic ride and a few expert kisses under the moonlight.

'No thank you,' she said bluntly. 'I trust you are not going to put the fare on my bill. I have amply repaid you for my carriage ride through the park.'

With a few devastating words she broke the spell that the summer's night had wrapped round them. The gossamer threads were snapped. She had put a million miles between them; the distance was unbridgeable.

His eyes hardened like ice and his arms dropped to his side. There was a dangerous calm about him that was frightening. She saw a tiny pulse throbbing in his tanned neck.

'You certainly make your feelings clear,' he said. 'Quite the shrew. And a very competent actress. I was quite taken in. For a few minutes I actually thought the school marm had a heart. My mistake. I even thought you might be harbouring more pleasant thoughts about me after being saved from a fate worse than death. Or did you fancy those two thugs? Perhaps that's what turns you on?'

Reah stifled a cry of protest. He was cruel. She let out her breath in a long quivering sigh. She had had enough of this day, this evening, this night. She was shattered.

'If you want to know about my dream,' she said, her gaze fixed on him with a nervous intensity. 'I think it's a premonition. I think it will come true.'

There was a finality in her voice as if she had accepted the awful fate in her dream. Now she had said it out loud, and it was no longer a hidden fear. It had become a tangible horror; real and waiting for the future.

'I don't believe in that kind of dream,' he said firmly. He took her chin between his hands and looked down at her with a fierceness that shook her body. 'Nor must you.'

Then he was gone, leaving her alone to face what was left of the night.

FIVE

Reah awoke with the memory of Ewart's kisses still warm on her mouth. She curled over in the big bed her cheek against the cool linen, wishing that a different Ewart, a loving Ewart was in her arms.

She regretted her cutting remarks but she could not apologise to him. Her pride was too fierce.

This morning she would be friendly but cool. She got out a bright pink shirt and cut off the hem; she snipped up a deep fringe to below her bust. Another screwy outfit, her father would have said.

Yesterday she had spoken her father's name. Now a pleasant memory had come unbidden to her mind. Was it because of Florence or Ewart? Were the two entwined, casting some magic over her?

Suddenly it was important that she put things right between herself and Ewart. She quickly dialled the number of Ewart's suite. There was no answer. Finally she put the phone down, remembering that he was out early yesterday morning.

Hurriedly she showered and dressed. She guessed where he might be...the flower market in the Piazzale degli Uffizi.

She remembered the carriage ride through the wide avenues of the Cascine gardens; she would have ridden to the stars with such a man. What was happening to her? It was madness.

Was she falling in love...? She did not know...perhaps this inner turmoil was the brink of love. But why this man who she knew had a cruel ruthless streak, who had already hurt her; yet every time she needed help he was there with certain tempered kindness and consideration. He did not seem to connect her with Stanford Lawrence, and she was not going to tell him.

The stall holders were busy selling flowers. The signoras in black frocks and aprons were buying flowers to put on the tables of their pensiones or trattorias.

She sought the head of cropped brown hair among the crowds. He was always so assured, so unshakable. He easily stood out; that extra height, the vigorous way he walked, the classy clothes.

She wandered up and down aimlessly, her anticipation evaporating. She had taken longer than usual to get ready. They could have easily missed each other in the maze of twisting streets.

She waited almost an hour, then hurried back to the hotel. Reception confirmed that Signore Morgan had gone out. She hid her disappointment. He would turn up, she told herself; he always did.

She steeped her mind in the atmosphere of Florence itself...the lime trees in the piazzas, balconied terraces overflowing with flowers, the Madonnas on every street corner, the dark turreted villas and narrow old houses still with square holes in their stonework. These holes were where beams of oak once acted as bridges between the houses. Acres of red-tiled roofs with ochreous walls jumbled together, planless; gardens grew over gardens; tall magnolia trees were on nodding terms with palms and pomegranates.

She kept expecting to feel a hand on her bare midriff and Ewart smiling mockingly down at her.

She kept in the shade, drank limone with crushed ice. Ewart would come soon. He could not be long now. He was busy; he had to work. She would see him at dinner and she would wear the moonlight dress. So the day passed and Reah could not wait for the evening.

She bathed in deep scented water, dressed carefully, taking a long time over her make-up. She did not want to arrive in the bar before him. He had to be there first, to turn and see her.

There was a wary look in her eyes. The day had been a strange one; one moment walking on air and the next so desperately alone she could have sat on the pavement and buried her head in her arms.

But her sketch pad was full of delightful scenes. Tomorrow she would go to the street of stationers and indulge herself by buying more lovely paper.

Reah walked downstairs, the silk chiffon pleats rustling demurely round her knees. She glanced into the dimly lit bar but Ewart was not there. The barman smiled at her; she passed by as if she had not been going there anyway.

She stood outside the hotel in the dusk of the evening, her heart fluttering in her breast. It had all gone wrong. Wildly her thoughts raced to street accidents... He could be lying unrecognised in some casualty ward...or ill in his suite unable to reach the telephone. She gasped as another awful thought hit her. The two youths might have seen him during the day, lain in wait and leaped on him in some alley-way.

'Signore Morgan?' she asked anxiously

at reception, trying to control her fears. 'Do you know where he is? Did he leave a message for me?'

'No, signora, there is no message.' They knew she was worried. The hotel staff had been watching her.

'Momento, signorina,' said the receptionist. He went into an inner office to talk to someone. Reah waited expectantly.

'Signore Morgan took the train to Milan this morning,' he said, returning.

'Milan?' Reah repeated, stunned. 'He took the train? I didn't know...thank you, grazie. Do you know when he will be returning?'

'No, signorina. He did not say.'

Reah walked away, shocked. Ewart had gone to Milan without telling her; letting her wait and hope. How cruel. That wonderful drive in the park meant nothing to him; he had been amusing himself. She had been right first time. An Italian Contessa would be much more his style.

Probably the Contessa had gone to Milan with Ewart. Supposing the Contessa had kept him at arm's length the night before, that would explain Ewart's eagerness to get his kisses elsewhere.

Reah shut her eyes. Her imagination was out of control.

'Ah, signorina, permit me. There is a moth caught in your hair. He thinks you are a flower...'

The tone was light, admiring, friendly. The owner of the friendly voice was a young man, tall with glossy black hair.

'Permit me,' he said again, flicking at her hair.

'A moth?'

'Si—there it goes.' He pointed into the darkness towards the climbing roses. Reah was not sure whether she saw anything.

'Thank you. Grazie.'

'Forgive my English. At school I am always looking out of the window,' he grinned.

'Your English is very good,' Reah assured him.

'It would have been better if my teacher had been like you.' His eyes were openly admiring. 'But she was old lady with hair done up in a cake.'

'You mean a bun,' said Reah, amused. 'Her hair was up in a bun.' She twisted her hair back with her hands. 'Like this?'

'Si,' he agreed, but shook his head at the same time. 'But she did not look like you. Scusi, signorina...my name is Giovanni da Cortona. Please you will have a glass of wine with me? I should be so honoured.'

His words were like honey to her ears. She knew she was being outrageously flattered but it was nice. Ewart had left Florence. He did not care whether she was on her own or not. Giovanni seemed a pleasant young man. She would have one drink with him.

Giovanni escorted her into the bar and found her a seat. He had charming manners and Reah allowed him to fuss over her. Was the draught from the door too much? Did she like red or white Chianti?

'There is a special wine you must try while you are in Florence. The rose...a dry pink wine...it is called Vinrosa di Torre de Passeri. You will like it.' The name of the wine rolled off his tongue like a poem.

Giovanni came back balancing a bottle

and two glasses, and dishes of olives and nuts. Reah took the dishes from his hands.

'A whole bottle?'

'But of course,' he grinned, mischievously. 'I wish to take a long time to get knowing you. Talking will make us thirsty. We will eat, drink, talk, make friends. Then I will take you for supper of the best pasta in Florence.'

'Oh, I don't know...'

'Scusi,' he said quickly. 'I am over my head meeting such a beautiful lady. I am afraid of losing sight of you.'

'Do you live in Florence?' Reah asked, deliberately changing the subject.

'Si, I am born Florentine.' There was unmistakable pride in his voice and a fierce gleam in his eye.

'It is a beautiful city,' she agreed.

'I am glad you like my city. My city only wishes all its visitors were as beautiful as you.'

Reah hid a smile. She had a feeling that this young man could turn practically any remark into a compliment.

Giovanni was the kind of company she needed to take her mind off Ewart's sudden departure for Milan. He was absurd and amusing, his fractured English adding charm to his conversation. He was about her own age, perhaps a year older. He told her that he was a goldsmith and had one of the shops on the ancient stone bridge, the Ponte Vecchio.

'Here are the shops of the best jewellers, goldsmiths and silversmiths. The workshops are so small, you could not swing a cat. Tomorrow you will come and see my shop? I will give you a beautiful necklace.'

'No, you really are most kind, but I could not possibly accept such a gift,' said Reah firmly.

'You will hurt my heart to the quickly,' he said, putting his hand over the offended organ. 'The necklace will look perfect on that slender neck. It is made for this very expensive Italian dress.'

Reah laughed softly. The pink wine was going to her head.

She found she had agreed to supper.

Why not, she thought? They might as well eat together, and Giovanni would know the best places. Giovanni escorted her from the hotel with obvious pride, taking her arm protectively. He liked to be seen in the company of rich, beautiful foreign women.

He took her to a cellar restaurant which was lively and crowded. Giovanni was greeted on all sides, admiring glances being thrown in Reah's direction. The Signora came out of the kitchen, with rapid words of welcome and smiles of delight that Reah was to eat with them. She gave them a discreet table in a corner, a candle flickered in a Chianti bottle on the red check tablecloth. Two carnations leaned over in a small vase.

'This is nice,' enthused Giovanni. 'The tortellini is a dream. You will like? You have no need to think of your figure.' His eyes travelled over her slimness.

'The treasure of Florence is not all from the ground,' he went on, waving his hands expressively. 'You must see the bird's eye. I will take you to the hillside of Bellosguardo, where the view is magnifico. We will climb the steps of the Campanile to see the rooftops of Florence.'

Reah smiled at the way Giovanni had taken over the organisation of her sight-seeing. The new bottle of wine was rougher than the pink, but Reah did not care. She was enjoying herself.

Giovanni leaned across the table and stroked her bare forearm. It was a soft caressing movement. He had long fingers with well-kept nails. She removed his hand, and he leaned back, grinning, his eyes lazily half closed.

'The so reserved English lady,' he teased. 'She sits like the Madonna of the Stairs, so serious. I long to arouse the passion of your heart.'

Reah was surprised that he compared her to Michelangelo's marble relief, but then if he lived here he would know all the famous treasures.

'Such beauty should not be wasted,' he went on ardently, his eyes openly admiring her figure. 'Such perfection is made to be loved by a man who is a passionate lover of women.'

Reah knew he was about to recommend himself as such a lover; she had allowed him to go too far. It had been easier to let the talking go on, and not to worry too much about what he was saying.

'Not me,' said Reah, briskly. 'I'm not waiting for a passionate lover of women. I don't care to be part of a collection. I'm waiting for a very special man.'

Giovanni misunderstood Reah, partly because the wine had taken any coolness from her voice, and it was warm and throaty.

'Carissima, carissima,' he said tenderly. 'You have found that special man.'

'But my husband would not approve,' she laughed, saying the first thing that came into her head. 'He is very jealous.'

He looked somewhat taken—aback.

'Your husband is a fool to leave such a beautiful woman alone,' he said with a careless shrug. 'If I had such a jewel, she would always be in my sight.'

He seemed not in the least perturbed

by the news that she might be married. Reah began to think of routes of escape. She took her hand away.

'Tell me about yourself,' she said quickly, steering the conversation into safer channels. 'Tell me about your family and your work. Have you any hobbies?'

'Hobbies?' He looked bemused.

'In your spare time, when you are not working.'

His eyes lit up. 'Of course,' he said with unashamed pride. 'Beautiful women and love are my hobby; I am much accomplished in these arts!'

Reah wondered if there was any subject he could not turn to love; but she was used to coping with a room of girls bent on not doing any work. She thought of her pupils with affection. They had been stunned when her father drowned. For weeks there were small anonymous offerings of flowers on her desk...a few primroses, a bunch of violets, wild cowslips picked from the Downs...they arrived unseen and she put them in jars around the art room as silent tokens of sympathy.

'Are you as charming to all your sisters?' asked Reah, making a guess as to the size of his family.

'Mamma mia! My sisters!' he exclaimed. 'They talk of nothing but love and babies and men. I cannot understand it.'

Giovanni was diverted and began to talk of other things, amusingly.

Reah could not help wondering if Ewart was dining in some sophisticated night spot with the elegant Contessa at his side sipping champagne.

'Now we will go back to your hotel, yes?' he suggested, finishing the last of the wine.

'I'll go back, alone,' said Reah.

'I will not allow you to walk in the streets. It is not safe. I will see you to your room,' he insisted. 'I promise only to your room, cara. And no more.'

Reah did not believe a word of his promise but she would feel safer if she got as far as the hotel. She would have to deal with him there.

Once out into the dimly lit street, his arms went swiftly round her. Reah pushed him away, breaking into a determined English stride in the direction of the Palazzo Excelsior.

He caught up and put her arm through his, holding onto her hand.

'Scusi, cara,' he pleaded. 'I am insensible about you. It is a madness. Forgive me.'

'I don't like people grabbing me in the street,' said Reah, her nerves raw from the previous evening's encounter. 'I thought I had made it quite clear that I am not looking for a romantic interlude. No lover, no man...understand?'

'Si...si.' It was all a game to him.

They went into the hotel foyer, a mask of composure on Reah's face. His fingers were in a limpet grip, curled round her arm. She did not want a scene in public, but she was embarrassed by his air of proprietorship and intimacy. 'The signora's key,' he said to the reception staff. There was not one raised eyebrow but Reah knew that they were watching intently.

'Thank you for a very pleasant evening, Giovanni,' she said loudly, her voice raised for their benefit. 'I'll say good-night now.'

'I promised...to your room,' he said, equally clearly.

Reah turned her head away, fast losing her composure. She was so distressed at being unable to outwit Giovanni that she did not notice a figure walk into the marbled foyer.

Ewart was drawn-faced, grim, hardly welcoming, but Reah was relieved to see him. She wrenched herself from Giovanni's grip and ran to him, her eyes alight.

'Ewart...Ewart, thank goodness. You're back.'

'You didn't waste much time,' he said coldly.

'What do you mean? I didn't know where you'd gone I was so worried.'

'Obviously,' he interrupted.

'I waited all day.'

'All day?' he repeated ironically. 'A whole day? I am touched by the length of your concern.'

Giovanni strolled over, confident of his youth and charm, Reah's room key dangling from his fingers.

'Darling...' he began, putting both feet

right in it with one word. 'I have your key.'

'Giovanni...this is my... h—husband,' Reah introduced Ewart awkwardly. Ewart's eyes narrowed into pools of darkness.

'Darling is coming with me,' said Ewart dangerously. He took the key from Giovanni's hand. 'She has a bill to pay.'

'What do you mean?' Reah demanded. She was the one who had been left all day without an explanation or a message. 'I'm not going anywhere with you.'

'Oh yes you are,' he said, pulling her close to him. 'Your husband, remember? It's time you settled your debt.'

She looked at the cold anger mixed with contempt in his granite hard eyes and a panic began to rise in her throat. A sense of desolation swept through her...not her Welsh knight whom she had thought so different from other men, not him too?

A small moan escaped her lips. She knew if Ewart kissed her, she would not be able to resist. The chemistry between them was too strong.

'Please let me go,' she said in a low voice, hating the huskiness which had invaded it. 'I don't want a scene.'

'This is quite mild compared to the scene I feel like making,' he flared. 'Do you deny you were taking that hotel romeo to your room?'

Giovanni was making a discreet retreat. He had no wish to be involved in unpleasantness.

'Of course I deny it,' said Reah. 'I was trying to shake him off. But what business is it of yours anyway?' she taunted him, her eyes flashing, hair aflame. 'I'm single, a free spirit. I can do exactly what I like.'

'No you can't. While you're here, you are in my care,' he snapped, with an arrogant tilt of his head. 'Come with me and don't argue.'

He turned and walked her firmly in the direction of the lift.

'No Ewart. Stop it. Don't make me do this,' she said, struggling. 'This is madness.'

'It didn't take you long to find someone else to buy your supper, did it? Well,

I'm tired of waiting. I want my payment now.'

He pushed her into the lift and the doors closed silently. She had never seen him look so angry.

'I'll pay you back, every penny. If you'll just wait until I'm back in England...'

'I don't want your money,' he said harshly. 'I make more money than I'll ever need. And don't play the little innocent. It's you I want...you and your damned red hair.'

He unlocked his door and propelled her inside. She stood wretchedly, hardly able to believe that Ewart could be serious. He slammed the door shut and turned the lock on the handle. He switched on a low lamp.

The suite was elegant and luxurious but Reah saw none of it. She saw only Ewart's blazing eyes and the powerful thrust of his shoulders as he shook off his jacket.

'Take off your clothes,' he commanded.

Reah froze, terror and confusion turning her to ice.

'Take off your dress,' he said coldly. 'Or do you want me to tear it off? I will you know. Then you'll have nothing to wear when you go back to your room. That could be very embarrassing.'

She began to tremble. This was not Ewart, the man who had kissed her with passion and gentleness in the Cascine gardens, whose love-making could be so tender. had she dreamed that romantic ride?

Button by button, he unfastened his shirt and pulled it out of his waistband. He strolled over to her and tipped back her head.

'Perhaps this'll warm you up,' he said huskily.

His mouth came down on her lips with a ruthlessness that sent shock waves reeling through her body. Her legs went weak as he pulled her against him. She tried to escape his mouth, turning and twisting, but he pursued her relentlessly, biting her soft flesh with an urgency that made her cry out.

'You liked that, didn't you?' he whispered. His face was in darkness, a stranger's face.

'No...no,' said Reah, blinking back her tears. 'You're being cruel and hateful. Please let me go. The joke's over.'

'Don't tell me that you don't want my kisses,' he said. He traced the line of her cheek with his finger, following it with kisses persuasive and caressing. She felt a warmth rising in her veins. His arms closed round her, his hands finding the soft curves of her body with an assurance and mastery that had her traitor body responding to his touch.

'Now take your dress off,' he said again.

She hardly knew what she was doing. She wanted him so much. This was her special man. She wanted to be loved by him, to belong to him. It was bewildering, the fury and the passion...none of it had any relation to her conception of love. This then was the real Ewart Morgan.

With a small sob, she fumbled with the fastening of the dress and it fell to the floor like a moonbeam. Her hair swung across her face as she stood motionless in her lacy bra and bikini pants. He was looking at her and she could not bear it.

Her breasts were rising and falling rapidly. He did not touch them but she could feel his breath on her soft skin. She ached with a sweet stab of longing to feel his fingers explore the valleys of love.

He tugged lightly at the edge of the lacy bra.

'That's a very wanton garment,' he said. 'Hardly the bra one would expect to find on a school mistress.'

He slid his fingers to the tiny satin bow at the centre; Reah held her breath at the exquisite pleasure. His other hand went to the small of her spine, jerking her so close that his fingers were trapped in the warm hollow between her breasts. A shudder went through Reah's body. He was discovering the quickly moving swell through the flimsy material; her senses were reeling, commonsense had flown leaving only a reckless urge for more of this ecstatic pleasure.

Ewart heard the low moan but did not kiss her, leaving her longing taut and aching almost unbearably. He knew how to arouse her, to tantalise her senses while holding himself in control. It was a demonstration of his strength and her weakness. It was as if he were mocking her frail body, while she could do nothing but surrender to the surging delight. She could not escape while his hands played such sensitive music. She was trapped.

Suddenly he dropped his head, taking her mouth with a thirst that would have sent her staggering if his hold had not been so unyielding. Her mind swam in a misty sea of images. There were stars, bright lights, swirling darkness. The muskiness of his skin was primitive. The shattering intimacy of his invading tongue left her breathless and shocked.

There had been nothing in her life before compared with this. All her deepest instincts responded to her growing desire. She wanted this man. He was her fate.

'To bed,' he said. His voice was like a whiplash.

She was quite unable to move. She thought she saw a different expression, fleeting and unfathomable, cross his face, but is was quickly replaced by a mask. He slipped an arm under her knees and jerked her across him like a doll, carrying her across to the bed. She fell onto it, gasping, but before she could move or regain her breath, the hard crushing weight of Ewart's body forced her back into its softness.

She began to weep as his kisses deepened, forcing her body to respond with slow shivers. His weight was forcing her legs to part, crushing her ribs, her arms flung outspread like a ritual sacrifice.

Suddenly the humiliation of this love-making rushed through her with all the force of a torrent. She gathered strength and caught him off guard with a quick, violent catapult movement of her knees. He rolled over, not in pain but definitely taken by surprise.

'No, I won't give in to you this way,' she cried, wrenching the sheet up and over her bare skin. Anger flared through her. 'How dare you use me to satisfy some animal instinct, to pay me back in some way. I'm a person, a real person and I won't be treated like this, not by you or by anyone!'

She gathered the sheet round her like an outraged Buddha, hardly knowing what she was saying or doing.

'I don't care who you are or how famous you may be. You've no right to force anyone or demand anything. You're no better than those two hooligans in the street!'

She was shaking with righteous fury. She scrambled off the bed, pulling the sheet after her, her fingers trembling as she draped it into a toga. She snatched her key from the side table.

'My father would have beaten the living daylights out of you,' she raged, her eyes spitting fire. 'You're just a brute, Ewart Morgan. No better than the mud and slime that flooded this city.'

Ewart was watching her from the bed. Suddenly he stretched out and lay back, clasping his hands behind his head.

'All right, go,' he said casually. 'I didn't really want you anyway.'

SIX

She was hurt and angry, scrubbing herself nearly raw in the bath. A sense of desolation swept through her slim body. Yesterday's happiness had been nothing more than a moment out of time, nothing to do with the real world.

At last Reah did get to sleep, curled up like a kitten; her bruised and disturbed emotions tossed her straight into the old terror dream of drowning. Now that she knew the identity of the man in her nightmare, it was even more horrific. She saw Ewart fighting against the waves that threatened to pull him under; his face disappearing with a startled look beneath the towering seas.

She struggled to surface from the dream, gasping, her face streaming with perspiration, reliving the feeling of suffocation. She ached inwardly for all that had happened in these recent months. Her father's death, the cruel and senseless way Ewart Morgan had hounded her through her solicitor, the strange and exciting chemistry between them, and now to have been used by him so wantonly. She did not know which hurt the most.

Early the next morning, she threw her belongings into her case. After last night she could not possibly stay.

She felt the need to make some symbolic gesture. A note did not seem appropriate.

She laid the moonlight dress on the bed and tore a sheet from her sketch pad and pinned it carefully to the dress. It was one of her sketches of the head of David, that handsome face with the hooded, troubled eyes, the frown, the concentration, the tight clusters of stone curls.

She was trying to say that the treasures of Florence were far more important than a romp in bed. If Ewart did not get the message, then it did not matter.

Reah walked confidently through the streets of Florence. She only needed a room for a few nights, and she had all day to find one herself.

This time she was lucky at her third call. The plump, black-frocked signora had a cancellation and was prepared to let the room to Reah for the remainder of the week.

Reah's bedroom was little more than a cupboard, but she felt immediately at home. The rooms in her cottage were mostly small.

Reah resolved to put Ewart firmly out of mind. She would forget last night and concentrate on sketching. She would build up her portfolio and plan a course for her students.

She had not drawn the Ponte Vecchio, the ancient 14th-century bridge—the only one the Germans did not blow up in 1944.

The bridge was a fascinating jumble of medieval architecture, stone compartments along the crenellated walls overhanging the river; impossible upper floors leaning out at crazy angles. It was Walt Disney long before Walt Disney.

Reah was good a buildings. She had a keen eye for perspective and composition, and her own particular style for conveying the texture of stone or brickwork.

She settled herself onto a step beneath a statue, her pad open on her knees.

'La bella signora, Buorn Giorno.' The compliment was slightly hesitant. Giovanni was looking at her shorn jeans and fringed shirt, not knowing what to make of them. Rich women had strange whims, and to look like a street urchin , even an adorable street urchin could be one of them.

'Hello, Giovanni,' said Reah. She had forgotten he had a goldsmith's shop on the bridge.

'I went to your hotel this morning,' said Giovanni, getting straight to the point. 'They said you moved out.'

'That's right. I didn't feel like paying the bill.'

Giovanni looked bewildered. 'You have left your husband?'

'He wasn't my husband.'

'Ah...' he nodded knowingly, pursing his lips.

'I made him up.'

Giovanni looked blank. Ewart had

seemed pretty substantial to him.

'I thought it was one way to curb your amorous advances. A husband in the background seemed a line of defence.'

Giovanni blinked his long lashes, astonished. 'To stop me? How could you? But, cara, surely you would have been deadly offended if I had not made the advances? What else can compliment a beautiful woman?'

Reah laughed, a delightful sound that brought a sparkle to her hazel eyes. 'You may find it hard to believe, but I would have preferred an ordinary, uneventful evening with a pleasant young man for company instead of having to fend you off after every mouthful.'

He looked crestfallen, then his face lit up. 'I was so attentive,' he grinned. 'Now you tell me I could have taken it easy.'

'No need to make it sound like hard work,' said Reah.

'So you are not married, not staying at the Palazzo, not looking for a lover,' he said with a big sigh.

'And not rich,' Reah added.

'Ah, triste...triste,' he said with mock sadness. 'Just when I am beginning to like you.'

'I am a schoolteacher. I teach art. This is a holiday and I work for my living, like you do.'

Giovanni put his hand on his heart dramatically. 'I am confessing also. One step along the bridge and you would have discovered my deceit. I am not a goldsmith. I do not own a shop, but one day I will. That is my ambition.' He grew inches with pride. 'Now I am...just salesman.'

'Thank you for telling me,' said Reah, now placing the dark suit accurately. 'I'm sure you will own your shop one day, especially if you are so charming to your customers.'

'Now I will ask you to be my date this evening. We will go dancing? You would like that? I can hold you in my arms and there will be no fighting off.'

Reah had not been dancing for ages. It might be fun, especially now that there were no pretences.

'I'd like that. Thank you.'

They arranged to meet at the Piazzo Duomo at eight o'clock when Giovanni had finished work and locked up.

Later Reah sat at a pavement cafe, sipping a limonata in the shade of an umbrella. It must have been one of the hottest days of the year. Male tourists mopped their foreheads with large handkerchieves; women fanned with straw hats bought in the market. The Florentines had mostly disappeared.

Reah watched a car coming along the street. It was being driven slowly which was unusual, the sun flashing on its huge chromium headlamps. Reah could see it was a vintage model of an Italian sports car, all dash and elegance with masses of shiny chrome.

'That's an Alfa Romeo,' said a man nearby. 'Worth a fortune, a car like that.'

But Reah was staring at the man in the passenger seat. It was Ewart, his face relaxed his arm resting comfortably along the edge of the open window. Beside him, driving, was a slim woman, sitting very

135

erect. Her face was hidden by enormous sunglasses, and her hair was covered by a cream silk scarf. She looked every inch a Contessa.

He was obviously enjoying the Contessa's attractive company, she thought, forgetting her own arrangements with Giovanni. She felt pretty sure he had not seen her.

Her face clouded as she thought of his demands last night. It was just as well she would not be meeting him. She would be tempted to tell him exactly what she thought of his behaviour.

She heard the empty chair at her table being scraped back and someone sat down. Her heart fell as she met the steely gaze in his dark eyes.

'Is this seat taken?' he asked, sitting down.

'It appears to be now,' she said curtly.

'You might be waiting for someone. You don't normally sit down for long. You dash about like frantic rabbit. So foolish in this heat. One should slow down and adapt.'

'I think I've heard this lecture before,' said Reah stiffly. 'Don't you have an alternative?'

'Don't tempt me,' said Ewart, beckoning a waiter. 'I have several lectures suitable for young women. Dos cafe freddo,' he ordered. 'You deserve a good dressing down.'

'Me?' Reah flashed dangerously. 'I suggest we leave the subject of last night alone if that's what you are inferring. I should enjoy telling you exactly what I think of you, and it might deflate your ego to the point of extinction.'

'I often wonder how you managed to become a school teacher. Don't you have to be an adult or something?'

Reah bit back her anger. There was nothing apologetic or conciliatory about his manner. He was looking at her as if she was the one in the wrong.

'Why have you run away?' he asked abruptly.

Her eyes widened with astonishment. 'Run away? I haven't run away. I've merely moved to a more agreeable residence. I had no intention of running the risk of a repetition of your despicable behaviour last night.'

'What about your own behaviour—blatantly taking a man to your room. I suppose you've moved to an area where such arrangements are less noticeable.'

'What rubbish,' said Reah fiercely. 'You're jumping to conclusions without knowing the facts. Giovanni was not coming to my room. He was merely escorting me to the door. There's a world of difference. I had no intention of letting him in.'

'He had your key,' Ewart interrupted.

'I admit he had the key,' Reah hastened to add. 'And he was holding my arm. I was doing my best to discourage him.'

'You were doing an excellent job of it,' said Ewart sardonically. 'The young man certainly got the message.'

'Oh don't be so stuffy,' said Reah. 'I wouldn't even have spoken to Giovanni if you'd had the courtesy to leave me a message. I didn't know you'd gone to Milan.'

'Why should you know,' he said. 'You're not my keeper.'

It was like a slap across the face. Reah was shaken by the coldness in his tone. Was this how he really felt about her?

'I know I'm not your keeper,' said Reah, trying to bring down the level of her voice. People were looking at them from other tables. 'But I waited around for you all day. You might have said you were going to be away.'

'There was absolutely no reason why I should have told you where I was going,' he retorted, glaring at her. 'Possessiveness is a trait I dislike in women. Give an inch and the next moment they are choosing your ties and redecorating your flat.'

'So the ride in the park was an inch of the famous playwright's attention, was it? How many inches are you allowing the Contessa? Do you have a scale according to status? A Contessa would rate pretty high up, I should imagine.'

'You do talk nonsense. The Contessa Birnini is a charming woman and I suggest you leave her out of this conversation.'

Reah gave a short laugh. 'Caught you on the raw, have we? I saw you in her car just now. That was her, wasn't it?'

'Yes, I'm not denying it. I was worried. I was looking for you. I was wondering what fool trouble were you in now.'

'You didn't look worried, sitting there quite relaxed and comfortable.'

'I found you, didn't I?' he snapped.

'You didn't appear to see me.'

His cold anger was mixed with exasperation. 'If I had started waving to you, you would have been off in a second. I suggested to Bianca that she drove round the corner and let me out there.'

'Bianca?'

'The Contessa. I'm a little tired of this third degree, Reah. And you haven't answered my original question.'

Tears pricked Reah's eyes. It was she who should be reproaching him for his brutal treatment; instead he had her on the defensive as if she was at fault.

'I can't argue with you,' she said bitterly, searching in her bag for money to pay for her drink. 'You turn everything round. I suppose your behaviour to me in your room was normal to you and nothing to be ashamed about. Well, I'm glad I live in a more civilised community where women aren't forced to give sexual favours, and we still believe in a funny old-fashioned thing called love.'

She rose awkwardly, knocking over what was left of the drink.

'I have no wish to see you again,' she said. 'So don't look for me and don't follow me. I'll send you money for the hotel bill if you'll kindly let me know how much.'

'Rubbish,' he said. 'Keep your money.'

'A gentleman to the very last,' said Reah with acid sweetness. 'I think I prefer statues.'

She managed an exit with elan despite the shorn jeans and fringed shirt.

That afternoon Reah bought a sketch pad and chose a pair of Florentine gloves for Miss Hardcastle. They were pale grey, in a suede so soft it felt like velvet.

She put on the eau de nil dress for her evening of dancing with Giovanni. It was a modest enough dress despite the slashed sleeves. She did not think there would be any problems tonight.

The motherly signora approved of Reah's outfit with much hand-clapping and smiles, but she insisted on lending Reah a lacy shawl. It was going to rain, she mimed, pointing at the sky.

'Grazie,' said Reah feeling obliged to take the shawl in the face of such concern. She realised it was old lace and probably quite valuable.

'Madre...grand-madre,' said the signora, smiling proudly and patting the shawl. She was lending Reah her grandmother's shawl. She trusted Reah implicitly.

Giovanni was waiting in the piazzo. His face broke into a grin and he hurried over to her.

'I thought you would not come,' he confessed.

'But I said I would.'

'I am not a rich suitor,' he said forlornly, obviously thinking of Ewart Morgan and the Palazzo Excelsior.

'For heaven's sake,' said Reah. 'We're

only going dancing. You don't have to be rich to dance well.'

Giovanni took her to Petit Bois, a little town on the outskirts of Florence, where there was an open air disco in the garden of a chalet.

They found a table under the trees, ordered some wine and soon they were on the floor dancing to the latest Italian disco beat. Reah enjoyed dancing, but there had been little opportunity since her student days.

Tonight Reah was careful not to drink wine as if it were water, and managed to order herself some limonata when the waiter returned to their table. She also insisted that it was her turn to pay.

Giovanni was faintly insulted, but Reah was firm. She did not wish to be under an obligation to him, or any man ever again. He accepted the situation reluctantly then forgot about it the moment the music began a slow dreamy love song.

She was in his arms before she had a chance to refuse. He had his arms twined around her, his face against her cheek, crooning softly in her ear. It was hopeless to struggle or try to dance a little less intimately.

She gave up and let herself relax in his arms. She would enjoy the gentle music and the nice feeling of his closeness. He was enthusiastic and romantic. A sign of being very young, thought Reah with amusement, feeling herself to be nearly a hundred years old.

'Carissima,' he sighed as the music faded away, but he did not loosen his arms. 'You are lovely. If only you were a little rich.'

Reah could not help laughing. He was incorrigible.

'So sorry,' she teased. 'Not even a little bit rich.'

At first no one heard the tiny pattering on the leaves as the sound was drowned by loud stereo music. A few drops fell through the leafy ceiling but the perspiring dancers hardly noticed.

Suddenly the pattering turned into drumming and the skies opened. A deluge poured onto the dancers and everyone ran shrieking for shelter. Reah was soaked in a few moments standing under a tree.

'What a downpour,' said Reah lightly. 'Do you think it's another flood?' The rain was dripping off her face and her neck.

'It is terrible,' said Giovanni gloomily, seeing his romantic evening literally going down the drain.

The deluge slowed but it looked as if rain had set in for the evening and the dancing was ruined.

'I'll find a taxi,' said Giovanni, suddenly brisk and practical.

He left her in the dark shadowy trees and Reah shivered. The signora's shawl was soaked. The only thing she could do was to hang it carefully from a branch of a tree and hope the worst would drain off. It was too delicate to wring or squeeze.

The music started again hopefully, but no one wanted to dance. People began to disperse, heading for home and dry clothes. Reah did not like being almost the last person left in the garden. She began to feel cold and shivery.

Giovanni came hurrying out of the darkness, waving his arms.

'Quick,' he called. 'I have a taxi! I cannot hold it for long.'

'Marvellous,' said Reah, relieved that he had come back at all. He led her through the wet bushes to a side entrance. A yellow taxi was waiting in the street.

'This is my friend,' said Giovanni, opening the door for her. 'He was at home in bed. There are no taxis anywhere.'

'It's very kind of him.'

'I am so sorry,' said Giovanni helplessly once they were in the taxi and driving away. 'The evening to end like this.'

'It's not your fault,' said Reah. 'It was a lovely evening until it started to rain. I was really enjoying it. The music was great and you're a very good dancer.'

It was like trying to cheer up one of her despondent students who had failed 'O' levels again. Reah did not mind the evening ending this way. The rain had dampened Giovanni's ardour and he attempted to do no more than hold her hand in the taxi.

Eventually the taxi turned into a street and drew up outside a row of small residential houses.

'I don't recognise this,' said Reah. 'Where are we?'

'This is where I live,' said Giovanni opening the door. 'Scusi, but I have to go. I have to dry and press my suit for tomorrow. It is necessary for the shop, you understand?'

Reah's heart filled with compassion for the downcast young man. The dark suit was his best and he had to make it presentable for work in the goldsmith's shop.

'Of course I understand,' she said and kissed his cheek in a sisterly way. 'Go in and get dried off. I'll pay for the taxi.'

'Buono notte, cara,' he said, returning the kiss.

She sat back, alone in the taxi, and began to laugh quietly. It was really too funny. She had been abandoned by her date and left to go home alone because he had to press his suit.

Soon Reah would be in her little room at the pensione; the narrow bed made up with heavy cotton sheets smelling sweetly of lavender; the comfort of dry clothes.

Perhaps the signora would allow her to make a hot drink in the kitchen.

Reah gripped the edge of the taxi seat. She had forgotten the signora's shawl in her haste to follow Giovanni. It was hanging from the tree like a ghostly cobweb, dripping onto the deserted dance floor. She would have to go back for it.

When she explained to the taxi driver that she wanted to go back he shook his head. He had only turned out because he was a friend of Giovanni's; he was not on duty; he would lose his licence; he wanted to go home. He would take her to her pensione and that was all.

'Finito,' he said, settling the matter.

Reah peered desperately out of the window. There was not another taxi around. It was as Giovanni said, they all disappeared with the rain.

The taxi turned into a wider avenue. Reah recognised the bright lights and imposing stone walls of the Hotel Palazzo Excelsior ahead. As they drove past she saw the gleaming headlamps of the Alfa Romeo parked outside. With a tremendous effort, Reah swallowed her pride.

The signora's antique shawl, so kindly and generously lent, was more important than any insults Ewart might bring down on her head.

'You can stop here,' said Reah before she could change her mind. 'How much do I owe you? Quanto e?'

She counted the lire notes and added a good tip.

She hurried into the hotel reception before courage could desert her. She knew she looked like something the cat had dragged in, but the reception staff were well trained and did not move an eyelid.

'Signore Morgan, per favore.'

'Si, signorina. Momento. I believe Signore Morgan is in the restaurant.'

Dining with the Contessa no doubt, thought Reah, her heart sinking. She stood in the foyer like a statue, dripping onto the marble floor, knowing that Ewart was her only chance. If she had to go on bended knee, then she would.

He came out of the restaurant, a linen napkin in his hand, dark blue velvet jacket unbuttoned. He looked at her dejected figure and gave a short laugh.

'I don't believe it,' he said. 'What has happened to you now? Have you fallen into the River Arno?'

'I'm very sorry to interrupt your meal,' said Reah in a rush, gathering her courage. 'Please say that you'll help me. I really need your help. You're the only person I can ask.'

'Help you? Why should I?'

'There are no taxis around and I've got to get the signora's shawl. I hung it on a tree. I know that sounds silly but it was raining and it was her grandmother's shawl and very valuable. I shouldn't have borrowed it, but she insisted and I didn't want to hurt her feelings. The taxi driver wouldn't take me any further because it was his night off, and there's no one I can ask but you...' she babbled incoherently.

'Stop. Stop,' said Ewart, holding up his hand. 'I don't understand a word. What's up a tree? Somebody's grandmother?'

'No, the shawl. It belongs to the signora where I'm staying. I must get it back...'

Reah was shivering, aware of the derision in his dark eyes, but beyond caring.

'You're frozen,' he said sharply. 'And you look like a drowned rat. You'd better change your clothes before you get pneumonia. Come with me.'

'No, thank you,' said Reah as he took her arm and propelled her towards the lift. 'I'm all right, really. You've got a guest.'

'If you want me to help you, then do as you are told and don't argue.'

As she walked she left a trail of raindrops across the floor. She tried to control the shivering as they went up in the lift in silence, but it was impossible. He took her into his suite, marched through to the bathroom and turned on the hot shower.

'Get out of those wet clothes,' he ordered. 'I'll find you something to wear.'

Reah darted into the bathroom and peeled off her wet dress and underclothes. The hot shower was a curtain of warmth, and she rubbed her limbs vigorously to bring back some feeling. She stepped out quickly and grabbed a bath towel as she heard the door open.

He glanced at her glistening skin, the draped towel almost slipping from her tautly tipped breasts. Reah clutched the towel to her throat.

'Don't you ever knock?' she asked with a small spurt of indignation.

'Not when it's my own bathroom.'

He tossed some clothes at her.

'These might fit,' he said. 'Put them on.'

The warmth of the water had revived her spirits and she towelled herself briskly. She glared at Ewart standing motionless in the doorway and turned her back to him. Damn him, if he was going to watch her. She would have to wriggle into the clothes as fast as possible.

'Don't worry,' she head him laugh sardonically. 'I won't look. I prefer elegant blondes, remember?'

She struggled into his expensive designer-made jeans. They were too large but she pulled the belt as tight as it would go. She slipped the fawn cashmere v-necked pullover over her bare skin and its warmth was immediately a pleasure. Her breasts moved against its softness, unrestricted by a bra, as she bent down to roll up the trouser legs.

She went through to his bedroom and into the sitting room. His typewriter was open on a table and everywhere was strewn with papers and maps. He had been working.

Ewart came over with a small glass of amber liquid.

'It's brandy. You need warming up inside as well.'

'Thanks.' She choked as the fiery liquid went down her throat. She felt waves of warmth spreading and tingling her body. The pure alcohol was very stimulating. She held out a bare foot.

'No shoes,' she said. Her sandals were sodden.

'I'm afraid I can't oblige there. You'll have to manage with a pair of socks.'

He found her a pair of blue socks and she sat on the floor to put them on.

'Let's get going. I've wasted enough time

this evening. I hope you know where this tree is.'

He held the door open. 'We'll take the Alfa.'

She looked slim and boyish in his clothes, her red hair slicked back so that her face was all great hazel eyes. His eyes were fixed on her face and she felt a sudden constriction in her throat, an unwillingness to meet his gaze.'

'Don't look at me like that,' she faltered. There was a restlessness in her body which could betray her.

'Do you find it disturbing?' he asked, striding ahead so fast she could hardly keep up.

'No,' she said vehemently. 'Just rude.'

'That's all right then. Get in,' he said.

Reah slid into the passenger seat in the big car. It smelt of leather and polish, and very elusively an expensive French perfume. The Contessa's perfume.

Reah crossed her arms, hugging the warmth. She hoped she remembered the way. She tried to gather her thoughts.

'It's a little place outside Florence called Petit Bois. An open air disco. I'll be able to recognise it.'

She had not realised it was so far. He drove silently, only stopping once to ask directions.

'So you've been out dancing with your Romeo,' he said at last, breaking the silence.

'Yes.'

'And where is he now?'

'He's gone home.' Reah was not going to tell him why. 'I only remembered later that I had left the shawl behind.'

'Why come to me?'

Reah swallowed. He was going to make her crawl. She supposed she deserved it.

'I was desperate and I couldn't think what to do. I had to get the shawl...I was prepared to...plead.' She blushed in the darkness. 'It's important because she trusted me with it. You were the only person in Florence who might help.'

The car was speeding out of Florence, the speedometer climbing. Rain glistened on the road; the patter of raindrops fell on the soft roof of the car as branches shed their load.

'Yes, I do have an amiable nature,' he acceded.

'I'm surprised they haven't awarded you the Nobel Peace Prize,' she said drily. The car skidded to a halt as Ewart stepped on the brakes. Reah was flung forward. He leaned across and put his hand on the door handle.

'Do you want to walk from here?' he suggested.

Reah sat up slowly, her pulses racing, pushing her hair out of her eyes.

'That was a very dangerous thing to do,' she said in a schoolmistress's voice, but she could not keep the tremor out of it.

'You make me do dangerous things,' he snapped back. 'Is that your disco over there?'

He pointed to fairy lights hung in the trees. The place looked deserted.

'Yes,' she said, getting out of the car. 'I can manage from here,' she added with a touch of hauteur. 'Thank you very much. You can return to the Contessa now. I'll walk back.'

'You'll do nothing of the sort. You'd only get lost or assaulted,' he said, following her into the disco.

The staff had almost finished clearing away. The chairs were stacked on tables. Someone was sweeping debris. No one had noticed the shawl hanging dejectedly from the tree. Reah ran across the floor, thankful to find it safe.

Perhaps they hoped Reah and Ewart were late customers, or they were playing music for themselves through the amplifiers, soft, seductive and quite bewitching.

Reah froze. The music was irresistible. The slow beat echoed the pounding of her heart; the guitar strings tore away barriers and reached out to the ache inside her slim body.

'They're playing our tune,' Ewart said lightly, taking her into his arms.

He did not hold her too close, but guided her slowly across the slippery floor. She had known he would be able to dance, and closed her eyes, forgetting that she was dancing in blue socks, moving in perfect harmony with this man. The man that she had first seen on the stairs; was it a million years ago? Images of Ewart floated through her mind...his granite dark eyes so serious, sometimes so deep in thought...then burning with passion as he kissed her...

Reah was hardly aware when the music stopped. Ewart gave her a little shake.

'Wake up, sleepy-head. It must be the brandy. I'll take you back now.'

She picked up the shawl and vaguely saw him tuck a note under an ashtray on one of the tables. The dance had been magical. She would never forget it. When she was grey-haired and still teaching, when other memories had faded, these moments in Florence would linger, warm and wonderful.

She told him where she was staying. The shawl lay damply on her knees as he drove swiftly and silently back into the centre of Florence. His face was etched against the darkness, gaunt and stern. She would remember him forever like a medieval knight's profile in stone in some ancient Welsh cathedral.

He stopped at the corner of the street, the engine still running. She longed for him to kiss her.

'Thank you, Ewart,' she said. 'That was very kind of you. I am grateful.'

He leaned across and opened her door. He was close and yet suddenly far away.

'I'll drop you here. The car might be difficult to explain to your signora,' he said.

'Yes. Good night.'

'Good night.'

His hands were back on the steering wheel and he was staring ahead, ready to pull out. He did not look at her. The big car moved away leaving Reah standing on the pavement.

'Your clothes...' she began but he was out of hearing, the car disappearing down the street and turning almost immediately. The red rear lights vanished. He had gone. It was as if he had gone from her life forever.

SEVEN

September in England began damp and cool. Reah put away her summer clothes, wondering when she would wear them again. She thought of the silvery moonlight dress, so beautiful and expensive. Even though it reminded her of that humiliating evening with Ewart, she could not help wondering who was wearing it now.

She had Ewart's jeans and cashmere sweater, washed, neatly folded and definitely in the way. She wanted to be rid of them. When the Autumn term began she would get his address from the college secretary.

Her last few days in Florence had flown. It had been impossible to see everything.

She had saved Michelangelo's 'David' for her last few hours in Florence. This enormous, almost overpowering figure deserved an hour of uninterrupted study.

It was a masterpiece of the first magnitude; a male figure of such strength and beauty. Her gaze was drawn to his face, to ponder on his troubled features.

She had been lost in a longing to have shared those moments with Ewart. She knew he too would have been deeply moved by the sculpture.

She stood at the bedroom window of her cottage at Southdean and remembered their enchanted carriage ride through the gardens of Cascine. How could he have kissed her with passion, held her closely with warmth and tenderness, then behave with such indifferent callousness.

With a sigh, Reah closed the window. Summer was over. She would forget Ewart as a distasteful memory.

Her flint-walled cottage was the end one of a terrace of four facing the village green of Southdean. The village nestled in a dip in the Downs and the sea was only a hill away.

Stanford Lawrence had bought the cottage long before he retired from the Royal Navy. It had been Reah's holiday home during her years at boarding school; then home for both once she left school.

Now the cottage seemed empty. Reah filled the air with music and the rooms with paintings, collages, bleached driftwood from the beach, pebbles polished to glossy blackness. She tended the garden with limited enthusiasm, not yet able to feel the point of growing things. The front garden was tiny with steps leading down onto the road; the back garden walled.

'Reah Lawrence?'

Reah held the telephone receiver against her shoulder in disbelief. It was the last voice she expected to hear. She took a deep breath to calm her clamouring pulse and return the receiver to her ear.

'Yes. Hello Ewart,' she said, surprised to find that her voice was steady.

'Are you well?'

'Yes, thank you.'

There was a pause. Reah wondered why he was calling; surely not out of concern for her health? The last words they had exchanged had been devastatingly final.

'Are you back to college yet?' His voice

sounded guarded.

'No. Ewart, I've a lot to do. Is this call important?'

Reah did not want to talk to him. Just hearing his voice was opening the half healed wounds, bringing back memories she wanted to forget.

'Of course it's important. Important for you. I don't make social calls. You should know that.'

She slid down onto an old flowered covered chair, slinging her legs over the upholstered arm. She curled her arm overhead and shut her eyes.

'Reah? Are you still there?'

'Only marginally. If this conversation does not improve in content, I may well fall asleep.'

She heard the deep familiar chuckle and her heart contracted. How could she ever forget that sound? Then he became brisk and business-like as if he had never kissed her, never held her closely in his arms.

'I'm having early planning conferences with my producer,' he said. 'My play is now in the scene planning stage. I've the actual dialogue to write. I've been thinking about the little sketches you made of life in Florence. Some of them were quite delightful,' he added quickly.

'We might be able to use them as linking material. Your sketch, then fade it into the actual building, statue or person. Then in reverse, say a shot of a fresco freezing into your simple sketch. What do you think of the idea?'

'I don't know.'

'What do you mean, you don't know? We'd like to have a look at your sketches. Could you bring them up to London?'

Reah's thoughts spun into confusion. Once she would have been delirious at the thought of her sketches being used in a television play, but now there were other aspects to consider. She wanted to keep out of Ewart's life; she did not want to see him again. She could not bear the thought of being anywhere near him...she might touch that cropped hair...his muscular leanness reminding her that he could melt her resistance.

'Reah—have you dropped off?'

'I can't come to London. It's out of the question.'

'Nonsense. There are plenty of trains from Eastbourne. Can you come on Friday? We'll have lunch somewhere.'

'I'm too busy. I'll post them.'

'That won't work. I need you to tell me the exact location of the sketches. The producer will be sending a camera crew to Florence, and he won't want to waste time.'

'No, I'm really sorry. It's not possible.'

She heard him exclaim with annoyance.

'Don't you want to see your sketches on television and your name in the credits? Miss Hardcastle would be proud of you. Think of your pupils...you'd score with them.'

'My students have different priorities,' said Reah. 'Television exposure doesn't rate too high.'

'There's a £200,000 budget for my play,' Ewart went on, ignoring her remark. 'There will be enough in the kitty to pay for your sketches. You could put central heating into your cottage. No more feudal fires.'

'How do you know about my central heating?' she asked, dismayed. Did he know everything about her?

'You talk in your sleep.'

'I don't believe you.'

'There's a certain artless ingenuity about your sketches that is a perfect contrast to the magnificence of the subjects,' he went on with devastating honesty.

'Childish, you mean.'

'I didn't say that. You said it. No, not childish, Reah; you are debasing your own innocent talent. Stop being so proud and stubborn. Surely your work comes before personal feelings?'

Reah was torn. She was tempted by the possibility of selling her sketches. It would be a purely business meeting.

'All right,' she said. 'But no lunch.'

'Would you care to conduct our business on the station platform? I daresay we could find a porter's trolley to sit on,' he mocked drily.

'Don't you have an office?'

166

'Oh yes, of course. All playwrights work in an office. I must get one. And a receptionist to make appointments. Perhaps you'd prefer to come to my flat?'

'No, thank you,' said Reah hastily. 'I'll leave you to arrange a venue.'

'Good. Friday then, at noon.'

'Yes, Friday.'

Reah was pleased about the sketches. She knew that they were not perfect, but that, it seemed, was why he wanted them. It was a crazy world.

She sat on the front door step of her cottage, huddled into a fleecy sweater and corduroy slacks.

The Japanese maple in her little garden was losing its rich summer colour. Reah loved the autumn too. And winter... blustery afternoon walks along the Seven Sisters trail with her father. Now there would be no one to talk to and she would have to walk alone.

Before she went to London, Reah had promised to show her sketches to Miss Hardcastle. It was nice going back to college; the gardeners tidying the grounds, the caretaker and his wife up ladders cleaning the windows.

Miss Hardcastle was also up a ladder, hanging new curtains. She looked pleased to have an interruption.

'Come in, Reah. I'm glad I'm going to see these sketches before Ewart Morgan takes his pick. Aren't you thrilled? It's exciting news. I knew you'd have a lovely time in Florence.'

'It's a beautiful city,' said Reah. 'But I can't say that Ewart Morgan's presence was exactly a bonus.'

'My dear, you're being sharp again,' said Miss Hardcastle with a twinkle.

'I kept meeting him. He seemed to think his mission in life was keeping an eye on me.'

'I wonder why,' said Miss Hardcastle vaguely. 'What time is your train? I don't want you to miss it.'

'We've plenty of time. Shall I make some coffee?'

'Lovely. You're looking very nice for your trip to town.'

Reah was wearing a black velvet suit and

an antique lace blouse that she had found in the Lanes at Brighton. It was Victorian with a high ruffled neck; a work of art with fine tucks and tiny embroidery. She had piled up her hair very severely so that the gaunt line of her cheeks was accentuated.

'You've lost weight,' Miss Hardcastle went on. 'That's not so good.'

'I haven't worn this suit since my father's funeral,' said Reah.

'Your father would have been proud of you,' said Irene Harcastle. 'Think of that instead. Your work on television.' She adjusted her half-moon spectacles and peered at the sketches. She could see why Ewart Morgan wanted them for his play. They were good. They had something...a kind of vulnerability that could only have come from the artist herself.

She glances at Reah obliquely. There was something different about her. The eyes had changed...the golden speckles in the hazel colour had deepened, were more glowing. Something had happened to make her grow up.

'These sketches really are very good,'

said Miss Hardcastle.

'I want you to have one,' said Reah.

'Of course I'd love one, but you've already given me the gloves, my dear. I'll wait until Ewart has had his pick.'

'No. Take one now. The play doesn't matter.'

'Reah, you must be sensible. The best must be for the play.' She had a sudden suspicion. 'Are they all here?'

'Yes,' said Reah. 'They're all there, except one sketch which I've kept for myself. It's of the head of David. It's... rather special.'

At last Reah stood up to repack her portfolio.

'I must go,' she said reluctantly.

'Off you go. Give my regards to Ewart Morgan and find out when his play will be on television. I wouldn't miss it for a ransom.'

'I don't think he's written it yet. These things take a long time,' said Reah with a wan smile.

Reah had no time to waste. She was cutting it fine for the train to London.

As she went out of the side door into the quadrangle, she head a short, sharp cry, an anguished cry of real pain.

Reah raced back up the stairs and pushed open the door. Miss Hardcastle was lying on the floor in an unnaturally twisted position, the ladder and curtains on top of her. Her face was ashen with pain.

'Go get your train...' Miss Hardcastle gasped. 'I'll be all right. Your train, girl...'

'What train?' said Reah calmly.

Three hours later Miss Hardcastle was tucked up in bed in Eastbourne General Hospital, her left wrist in plaster, and under observation for possible concussion. Reah had gone with her and stayed until she was settled comfortably.

She did not know where to contact Ewart to explain. His telephone was ex-directory. She did not know the name of his producer.

Miss Hardcastle was upset that she should have missed her appointment.

'If he's really interested, he'll get in touch,' said Reah. But she knew he wouldn't. Ewart was too proud to ask her again.

It was almost with a sense of relief that Reah let herself into her cottage that evening. How differently she had imagined this return from seeing Ewart. She hung away her velvet suit and changed into jeans and a jersey.

The day before term started Reah went for a long tramp along the top of the Seven Sisters towards Beachy Head. She took the National Trust trail along the Cuckmere estuary towards the white virginal sister called Haven Brown, using the natural steps in the rising path to keep a grip on the steep turf.

Below the waves had cut a platform into the shingle, and littered the shore with a debris of gulls feathers, nets and driftwood. Sea kale and the yellow horned poppy grew along the cliff path; the tiny red bartsia underfoot like moss. Stonechats and yellowhammers darted about for insects among the long coarse grass and scrub on the top of the cliff.

Reah stopped and turned at the top of the climb, to catch her breath and to take in the glorious view across the estuary. The River Cuckmere flowed through the salt marshes which were covered at most high tides; the lake and bird islands were peaceful sanctuaries surrounded by rolling hills and fields.

A dominant south-westerly was blowing at the top of the cliff, whipping Reah's hair across her face, billowing out her anorak like a balloon. It was not cold, but exhilaratingly fresh and blustery.

Reah could just make out the medieval earthern bank built to prevent flooding, the protective moat for the birds, and more recently the concrete anti-tank blocks from World War II.

Reah turned to continue her climb. Above her a figure was coming over the brow from the other direction. It was like an instant replay. She had seen it all before. Now it was the steps cut into the cliff path that he took so confidently and with such vigour.

His fringed hair was blowing in all

directions. He wore a brown leather jerkin and roll necked jersey. His hands were deep in his pockets, thoughts miles away.

Reah's heart quickened. It betrayed her every time she saw him. Feeling surged through her body, stabbing her with wild longing.

'Mr Morgan,' she said. 'What a coincidence.'

'Coincidence?' He looked at her vaguely, as if barely able to recognise who she was.

'Yes, coincidence. What a coincidence meeting you here.'

'Not really,' he said, looking at the view over her shoulder. 'I live here.'

'No, you don't. You live in London. You've got a flat. I remember you telling me.'

'My dear girl, I ought to know where I live and at present I live over there.'

He took her arm in a forceful manner and turned her in the direction of the farthest side of the mouth of the river. Two small houses perched on the lower cliff edge. One day there would be a rock fall and the cottages would go. They had already lost their gardens to the sea.

'The old coastguard cottages?'

'I've rented the empty one for a few months. I need somewhere quiet to write my play but near enough to London if there's a meeting. My flat is being redecorated and they are modernising the lift. I couldn't wait to get away. I moved in yesterday.'

'But why here?'

'I turned the car due south and drove. This suits me. I can get to London easily.'

'Well, I'm sure you'll get all the peace and quiet you need down here,' said Reah, making as if to continue her walk.

'Hold on, Reah,' he said, catching her arm. 'Don't you want to say anything else?'

Reah looked at him blankly.

'Don't you owe me an apology? I waited a whole hour.'

'I'm sorry,' said Reah. 'I couldn't telephone you. Miss Hardcastle broke her wrist and I had to stay with her.'

'Of course.'

He dropped her arm, and jogged a few yards down the path. Reah hesitated. Alarm bells were ringing in her head, and she had the feeling that if she let him go, she would regret it for the rest of her life.

'Is that all you've got to say?'

'I'm not a schoolteacher. I didn't ask for a four page essay on why you didn't turn up. I write plays that have to be 49 minutes and 30 seconds long. I thought your explanation was adequate.'

He came level with her, eyes narrowed against the glare of the sea; she could not tell the expression.

'Where's your hat?' he asked.

The question took Reah totally by surprise. He remembered her old Trilby, guessed why she wore it. How could he understand the depth of her grief when he had himself added to her distress? They had to clear the air between them. It was time he knew who she was.

She studied his face intently, trying to see answers in his dark eyes, the tiny mole, the sensitive mouth, the blowing hair.

'I suppose you've no food if you've just moved in.'

'No. Shopping was next on my list.'

'I can offer an omelette and green salad.'

'A gastronomic delight,' he said with a gleam. 'I'll get a bottle of wine from the pub.'

It was a strange feeling showing Ewart into the cottage, knowing that it would mean a confrontation. Now he would understand her anger. He looked round the comfortable room approvingly, then his gaze was riveted to the row of silver cups and photographs of her father. He walked straight to them.

'Stanford Lawrence,' he breathed.

There was a colour photograph of Captain Lawrence in naval uniform, his cap tucked under one arm, his red hair streaked with grey, eyes fearless and penetratingly honest. Reah's eyes.

'Your father was Stanford Lawrence, the lone yachtsman?' He could not keep the astonishment and awe out of his voice.

'Yes, you've heard of him, haven't you?'

'Of course, who hasn't? Why didn't you tell me, Reah? Stanford Lawrence...what a man. So Leslie Lawrence is your brother?'

'No,' said Reah, with an inexpressible feeling of sadness. 'Leslie Lawrence is not my brother. I don't have a brother. I'm Lesley Lawrence. My father christened me for the son he never had. Reah is my middle name and everyone calls me Reah. The newspapers got it wrong, but there was no point in correcting their story. My father was dead. What did it matter whether he had a son or a daughter?'

Ewart groaned, his hand to his forehead. 'My God, no wonder you hate me. I understand now. I could never fathom why you disliked me so much. I know I've got a wicked sarcastic streak, but what had I done? We would be getting on well, then suddenly it was like a curtain coming down. You just shut off from me, and there was no way of getting through to you. It was driving me mad. I can only say that I'm sorry. Can you forgive me?'

'No, I can't,' Reah cried with a rush

of indignation. 'I can't forgive that way you hounded me, day and night, all those letters and phone calls. How could you be so callous? My father had only been dead a few days and you were already offering me money for his story.'

He caught her hand in a tight grip. 'I know it must seem heartless to you, Reah, but truly time was important. I had admired your father for years. His war record, those long voyages alone, the time he drifted for days 4,000 miles from Cape Town without any provisions...I wanted to write about him. I didn't want anyone else to get there before me and get the rights to his story.'

Reah's anger spilled over. 'He wasn't a story,' she shouted. 'He was a person, a man! You don't sell a person. You don't sell your dead father. How could you, when I was so distraught, so upset? All I got was letter after letter, insisting that I should do this, or do that.'

Ewart linked his arms loosely round her waist. She arched away from him but he was like a rock.

'I didn't know it was as bad as that, Reah. My agent had no instructions to bully you.'

'Your agent?'

'Yes. I wasn't writing to you. It was my agent. I have an agent who sells my work, gets work for me. I asked him to get the rights from Stanford Lawrence's son—Leslie Lawrence.' He paused thinking back to the actual moment. 'I remember saying something like I wanted to do the play at all costs, but I meant at all costs to myself. I had so much on my plate, but I would do it even if it meant giving up something else, working day and night. He must have taken it to mean to get the rights at all costs. Perhaps that's why he was so insistent.'

He touched her chin with the merest thread of a caress. Reah felt the burden of hatred roll off her shoulders. She believed him.

'What about the phone call in the middle of the night?' she faltered, but the anger had gone out of her voice.

'My agent told me that you were refusing

to answer our letters. I was desperate. So I telephoned. Unfortunately I was in New York and forgot it was after midnight. I seem to remember you hung up on me,' he chuckled.

'You bet I did. I didn't want to speak to you. And I never wanted to mention the subject again. That's why I never told you who my father was,' said Reah, her eyes bright with tears. 'This afternoon on the cliff, I had a k—kind of message. The sea was glittering and it was like Morse code...I thought about how I had lost my father and...and...'

'No more,' he said gently, rocking her in his arms. 'How very hard this has been for you. To bear alone. But you're not alone any more. I am here.'

He was touching her face with infinite tenderness, tracing the high line of her cheek bone, down to the soft trembling curves of her mouth. Reah felt herself yearning for his touch. He was bringing her alive.

'Your father was one of the bravest men of his time. Take comfort from that;

strength, determination, will-power. All his qualities.'

She nodded. 'He was on the North Atlantic run at the beginning of the war, an escort destroyer on convoy duty. He survived all that. Then the lonely long-haul sailing with so much danger every day. And he dies in a sudden squall off Shoreham. It doesn't seem possible that he should live through so much then perish in some freak weather.'

He heard the racking pain in her voice. It was unanswerable.

'I don't know the right words,' he said. 'I don't think they exist. But from what I've read about your father, I'm sure that a sudden squall was a preferable end to months in hospital or the inactivity of an old people's home.'

'It was a new sailing boat,' Reah went on. 'It was a new design and he called it Reah. His enthusiasm for the boat was like an extension of loving me. I feel responsible...' her voice trailed away.

He pulled her roughly to him, his hands thrust through her hair, his cheek against her head. She could feel his body iron hard against her softer, yielding flesh.

'Reah, Reah. You must start living. Your thoughts are dominated by the past. Life is what's important. Life like this.'

His voice was husky as his mouth came down on her lips, till her neck ached with the pressure. She was living for his touch, returning his ardent kisses; her body hungered for him. All her old anger turned into a melting desire.

His fingers traced the fine line of her jaw, down her neck to the small hollow of her throat. He was bringing her alive with a gentleness that belied all the toughness of the man she once hated.

Ewart put his arms under her knees and lifted her up into his arms. She felt her heart beating suffocatingly.

'I don't think I can carry you up those narrow stairs,' he said against her hair. 'But that couch looks like heaven.'

He laid her gently on the cushions, twining his arms round her and turning her face so that he could reach her lips. She wanted him so dreadfully; all sense had left her. She could no longer think coherently. All she wanted was to be loved and loved by Ewart, even it if was only this once.

'Love me, love me...' she murmured wildly.

She felt him push her away. There was air between them where before their bodies had been so close. He brushed her forehead with his cheek, lightly, softly.

'Not yet, little one,' he said. 'That was just a taste of things to come. I promise you.' He looked deeply into her eyes as he repeated those words. 'I promise you, Reah. One day I will love you as no man has ever loved a woman.'

EIGHT

Supper was pleasant. Both Reah and Ewart were relieved from making a commitment they were not yet ready to make.

Afterwards Ewart saw her sketches.

'I've already prepared the treatment,' he said. 'That's planning the number of scenes. Every time there's a change of location, it means a new scene number, even if the shot is only a few seconds long.'

Reah felt a thrill of excitement. 'And you plan to use my sketches to link the scenes?'

'I want a build up of tension leading to the disaster of the flood. Your little sketches stop the action, ask a question, make a statement, giving the viewer glimpses of what's at stake.'

'Have you started the writing?'

He shook his head. 'It was hopeless. Pneumatic drills, hammering, the phone. I had to get away. I need a few weeks alone, to work like fury, to write it all in one concentrated effort.'

He left early, giving Reah a friendly kiss on the cheek as if those moments of passion had never been. She watched him walk away as she had so many times.

She collected up the remainder of her sketches from the floor and put them away.

Ewart had taken what he wanted. A cheque would arrive through the post. She would have her central heating before the winter came.

Her head was beginning to ache. She knew it was tension. She had never expected to see Ewart again; now he would be living almost on her doorstep.

Suddenly she remembered the package of Ewart's clothes, laundered, pressed and ready for return. She ran to the cottage door and called into the dark.

'Ewart, Ewart, come back.'

But he was out of earshot.

That night she could not sleep, remembering Ewart's warm body against her and his passionate kisses. She waited for morning to come, knowing that work was the only way to erase him from her mind.

The Autumn term started and Reah went back to college.

'Are you all right, Reah?' Miss Hardcastle's broken wrist was still in plaster, cradled in a sling made from a folded silk scarf. She was carrying an awkward pile of registers under her good arm.

'Let me take those,' said Reah. 'Where to?'

'My office. How do you like your new classes?'

'Fine. Quite a mixed bunch this year but I'm sure they'll soon shape up. And I want to try out some new ideas—if you don't mind, Miss Hardcastle?'

'You know I don't interfere with your department. As long as you are not planning a series of murals on the conference hall walls.'

'What a good idea,' said Reah with a twinkle. 'I hadn't thought of that. Southdean through the Ages—something like that?'

'I think it might take some explaining to the governors.'

It was dusk before Reah left college and was able to take the package of Ewart's clothes down to the coastguard's cottage. She walked along the Cuckmere river path, the wild fowl and migrating birds flocking for the night on the islands. The sea was pounding the shingle beach, the ozone fresh and invigorating.

She would hand him the package and the cheque to cover her debts, then retreat quickly. He would not want to be disturbed.

As she climbed the stony path to the red brick and stone cottage, she was unprepared for what she was about to see.

Outside the cottage, parked on the rough road, was the gleaming maroon Alfa Romeo, the car belonging to the Contessa Bianca Bernini.

Reah stumbled, clutching the parcel to her breast. Her heart was thudding violently. The Contessa had followed Ewart. They were together now.

Reah ran the last few yards, her head spinning, her vision blurred, feeling the way along the uneven path to the trellised porch. She put the package on the doorstep and fled.

She did not know how she got back to Southdean, tears scalding her eyes, her thoughts wild and disturbed. She had been a fool. The famous Ewart Morgan had just felt sorry for her.

The Alfa Romeo was the seventh wonder in the village for days. Reah got heartily sick of hearing about it. Everyone was talking about that 'furrin car and that television chap'. It did not look as if Ewart was doing much work.

Miss Hardcastle suspected that Reah had found more to her liking in Florence than its art treasures.

'I'm going to have a party,' said Miss Hardcastle, as if she had been planning it for days, whereas she had just thought of it. 'A thank-you to the people who have been so kind to me since I broke my wrist. There's the ambulance men and that nice young doctor; the nurses at the hospital; the caretaker and his wife. You, of course. You were a tower of strength that afternoon. And there's Ewart Morgan; he's almost a neighbour now.

'Ewart? Why Ewart?' Reah interrupted. 'He didn't do anything to help.'

'Only indirectly. After all, if he hand't invited you to London that day, you would

189

not have called in here first with your sketches. I might have lain undiscovered for hours.'

Reah felt prompted to say rubbish, but the look on Miss Hardcastle's face forbade it.

'Besides, he sent me lovely flowers when he heard about my accident,' Miss Hardcastle went on, with a twinkle in her eyes. 'I was very touched. What do you think about next Friday evening? Would that be a good time?'

'He won't come,' said Reah. 'He's writing his play. And he's got a visitor.'

'He can't write all the time. He must take the odd hour off to recharge his resources.'

'He's recharging his resources all right,' said Reah in an aside.

'I'll write the invitations this afternoon. Would you be able to take his invitation after school?'

Reah saw no way out. Miss Hardcastle would be offended if she did not turn up at the party. It would be ungracious not to do this small errand.

After school Reah cycled down the rough lane to the coastguard cottages. She propped her bike against a bank and ran up the short path to the door. It opened and Ewart stood in the doorway.

'I thought a juggernaut was approaching, or a Berman tank,' he said.

He was in his shirt-sleeves. His hair was tousled and a five o'clock shadow darkened his grim jaw.

'Where have you been?' he asked, catching her wrist. 'I haven't seen you for days.'

'You're supposed to be working,' said Reah.

'I am working. That's why I wanted you to call. I've no time to cook or eat. At least you could make me coffee.'

'What a nerve,' said Reah. 'Get your lady-friend to feed you. I'm sure she makes superb lasagne.'

'Get in and fix some coffee,' he said, propelling her inside. 'And don't touch any paper. I know where everything is and I want it to stay that way.'

The inside of the cottage was a sea

of paper. Sheets of typing lay on every available surface. An armchair was drawn up to the fire with a rug thrown over it. He had not even been to bed.

Reah put the invitation on the mantlepiece standing it against the clock. Spray spotted the windows facing the Channel and a loose sash cord rapped on the shutters.

'Don't forget to open it,' she said. 'Miss Hardcastle would be hurt if you didn't answer.'

His eyes strayed to his typewriter. His work was already pulling him back.

'Okay,' she sighed. 'I'm a fool. I'll make you some coffee.'

Reah disappeared into the kitchen to clear up the chaos. It took a while till everything was to her satisfaction. It was dark now; the sound of waves crashing on the shingle below was loud and fearsome. She would not like to live so near to the cliffs.

She made sandwiches and coffee then realised that the clatter from his typewriter had stopped. He had fallen asleep across the machine, his head cradled on folded arms. His face was turned towards her in the shadow, eyelashes like dark fans on his cheeks.

'Ewart...Ewart,' she spoke softly into his ear.

'Mmn?'

'Stand up and come with me.' She put her arms round his waist and hauled him into a standing position. She held him against her, panting a little with the exertion.

'This way,' she said in a schoolmarmish voice. 'Come along now. Walk.'

She hauled him across the room. He collapsed into the armchair almost taking Reah with him. She prised herself out of his arms and straightened up. He was sound asleep, sprawled over the chair, his head thrown back so that the dark hair of his chest showed at his unbuttoned shirt.

Ewart's face settled deeper into sleep, the tension disappearing. She eased off his sneakers and put his feet up onto a low stool. She fixed the old fashioned fire guard in front of the glowing coals, hoping the room would keep warm for a few hours.

She made a cheque out to Ewart Morgan leaving the amount blank, and put it with the invitation, propped against the clock. Now she did not owe him anything.

A terrible ache swelled inside her. She longed to have him sleep in her arms, his body folded against her, his head on her breast.

She touched his hair gently. It was soft as she had known it would be. She moved the fringe out of his eyes, then, trembling she bent and kissed him. All her love for him came into being and was recognised in that one sweet kiss on his sleeping face. She touched the tiny mole at the corner of his eyes, then left.

It was dark and blowy outside. She turned her bike into the tip of the wind and started to push it home. Her mind was in shattering confusion, knowing that she loved him.

There might never be another day. She scarcely recognised landmarks she had known since a girl.

Miss Hardcastle's party created a minor clothes problem for Reah. Cocktail parties, even rural ones, were not the normal social scene in Southdean.

Reah was almost resorting to a flying visit to the shops at Eastbourne when she remembered a length of flame-coloured tapestry she had bought to make new curtains for the sitting room and to re-cover the chairs.

The night before the party Reah sacrificed the chairs and made herself a full, gathered skirt from the material. With her antique blouse, narrow gold belt and strappy bronze sandals, it was a flamboyant outfit.

'This is such fun,' said Miss Hardcastle, who was wearing her prize-giving royal blue silk. 'I can't think why I haven't done it before.'

'Because you haven't broken a wrist before,' said Reah.

'Well, I shan't wait until I break a leg to have another party. Perhaps there'll be an engagement to celebrate, or something,' she added with a sly look.

It had grown into a big party. Cook had produced trays of canapes, cheese and curry dips with raw vegetables for dipping, and a mouthwatering selection of tiny eclairs, rum babas and meringues.

Reah was over by the window, talking to a school governor when Ewart arrived. She knew without turning that he was in the room.

His eyes were raking over her. The gold leather belt showed off her slimness and she knew that her small breasts, now rising more rapidly, were too clearly defined against he fine lawn of the blouse.

Suddenly he was at her side. She did not have to look.

'Will you excuse us,' he said politely to Reah's companion. 'I have an urgent matter to discuss with Miss Lawrence.' He took her arm and Reah saw, with a moment of chilling apprehension, that Ewart was not in a party mood.

She had never seen him so angry, yet cold at the same time. His eyes were dark and menacing.

'What the devil do you mean by this?'

Her blank cheque was crushed in his hand.

'It's the money I owe y-you,' she stumbled over the words.

'Everytime I think we are beginning to get along you do and do some damned fool thing to spoil it.'

'Me?' said Reah, indignantly, her wits returning. 'I didn't force myself into your room that night in Florence. I don't remember tearing off your shirt or holding you down on the bed. That's the kind of behaviour that spoils a relationship. Paying back owed money is hardly anti-social.'

Miss Hardcastle appeared with two glasses of sherry.

'This is a party, not an arena.' she said lightly. 'If you want to fight, go out into the quadrangle.'

Ewart was immediately contrite.

'I'm so sorry, Miss Hardcastle, but there's something about this obstinate young woman that sets my teeth on edge.'

'And I find television celebrities quite impossible to talk to rationally,' said Reah, sipping the sherry quickly to calm her jangling nerves.

'Then I suggest, Reah, that you go and talk to that nice young doctor from the hospital. Ewart, there are a couple of nurses longing to meet you. They seem to know all your plays.'

Miss Hardcastle moved on, hoping she had defused the situation. It was possible neither of them could see what was plainly obvious to her.

'Nice looking nurses,' said Ewart. 'Feminine and womanly. I can't bear skinny women, all bones and brains, ready to argue about everything.'

'Drop a few names, and they'll be swooning at your feet. I'm sure you know how. I shall enjoy meeting the doctor. People with worthwhile jobs interest me. Stringing together a few words of one syllable is hardly work.'

Ewart was incensed. Reah know she had gone too far again, but it gave her a heady surge of triumph. She wanted to hurt him.

He turned on his heel, helped himself

to an asparagus canape and spent the rest of the party being extremely charming to everyone except Reah. He said not another word to her.

Reah stayed behind to help clear up when the guests had gone. She did not notice Ewart leaving. Miss Hardcastle drifted around feeling a little high on three glasses of sherry and the euphoria of a successful party.

'I did enjoy myself,' she said, scraping out the last of a cream dip with a broken crisp. 'We ought to have more parties. What a pity you don't get on with that handsome Ewart Morgan.'

'I feel nothing but distaste for him.'

'That's a pretty skirt you're wearing.'

'My sitting-room curtains.'

'I'm sure Ewart Morgan noticed.'

'He wouldn't notice if I was wearing an ex-army bell tent,' said Reah stonily.

Reah left Miss Hardcastle sitting by the fire with a tray of tea, the clearing up finished and her flat ship-shape. She felt exhausted. She retrieved her bicycle and began to push it down the drive.

A tall man came out of the shadows; Reah was too worn out to be alarmed.

'I'll take you home,' said Ewart. 'You can't ride a bike in that skirt.' He bent nearer and sniffed. 'And you've had too much sherry.'

'Gallons,' said Reah.

'Don't exaggerate. The car's at the end of the drive. Leave your bike in the shrubs.'

He grasped her hand. She felt drained of emotion. The Alfa Romeo was at the entrance to the drive. Ewart had taken the nurses back to the hospital then returned for Reah.

'So the Contessa is back,' she said. 'I hope the menu has improved.' She could hardly trust herself to speak.

'The Contessa? Here, in my chaotic cottage? You over-estimate my appeal, dear girl. I doubt if that aristocratic lady would come within sniffing distance.'

He jerked her chin up. 'Nor would she care to leave the many children and grand-children who inhabit her villa outside Florence in droves.'

'Grand-children?'

'The Contessa Bianca Bernini is one of those wonderfully preserved Italian women who look forty but must be at least sixty. She is still beautiful and youthful. And she is something of a heroine. During the flood disaster she drove from the villa every day with her car full of food from her kitchen and produce from her gardens and set up free feeding points. Her sheets were torn up for nappies; she gave away every blanket she possessed. When the restoration work began, she and her children came every day, armed with blotting paper and talcum powder and worked painstakingly on the muddied lumps that were rare manuscripts and books.'

Reah's thoughts spun as she re-adjusted this new information.

'But Milan?' she asked.

'Another hero. The Contessa heard that this man, an ordinary shopkeeper, now old and retired, was visiting Milan just for the day. She phoned me and I went immediately to see him.'

'When I saw the car...I thought that...'

'The car is mine. The Contessa was in financial difficulties and I offered to buy the car from her. A simple transaction.'

Relief flooded through Reah making her dizzy. It was Ewart's car. The Contessa was not some man-eating Italian beauty, but a silver-haired grandmother tearing up sheets for nappies. Reah was ashamed of the thoughts that had become twisted and bitter in her mind.

'How could she bear to part with it,' said Reah in a low voice.

'Her late husband was a collector of vintage cars,' Ewart grinned. 'There are another four in the garage.'

He drove the big car carefully through the narrow lanes, its headlamps lighting up ghostly trees and hedgerows. He stopped near her cottage and switched off the engine. He turned to her, his arm casually along the back of the seat.

'Do I get a cup of coffee?' he asked.

'Yes, of course.'

Reah hurried ahead, Ewart close on her

heels. He caught sight of the flame-coloured tapestry material piled on the floor.

'Going in for mass production?' he asked pleasantly.

'My new curtains,' said Reah, bundling up the material.

'Do you often go to parties wearing your curtains?'

'Frequently. It gives me a sense of continuity.'

She made some coffee and opened a packet of chocolate digestive biscuits, taking it through to the sitting room on a tray. Ewart was sitting in her father's armchair. It was the first time she had felt comfortable about seeing someone else in it.

'The way to a man's heart,' said Ewart, helping himself to a biscuit. 'Tell me, Reah, since we haven't fought for at least ten minutes, what is the way to a woman's heart?'

'I'm not sure,' said Reah, stirring her coffee. 'Many things...humour, kindness, compassion, sensitivity, concern. It's two contradictions—strength and gentleness. A man must be both strong and gentle.'

He had lit the fire while she was in the kitchen, and it was beginning to throw out a rosy glow. 'Sit by me,' he said, indicating the sheepskin rug in front of the fire. 'It's the warmest place.

'I always used to sit like this with my father.'

She leaned against his knees. It seemed the most natural thing to do. He moved his legs so that she would be more comfortable.

'Perhaps you'd also like to tell me now why you look at me with such fear in your eyes?'

The question exploded in the quiet room like a bomb shell. Reah caught her breath. It was so unexpected. She hung her head, her escaping hair hiding her face in the firelight.

'Don't ask me that,' she said.

'But I must,' he insisted. 'I must know why you are afraid of me.'

She stared into the flickering flames, the horror of that night returning with force. She could see crashing waves in the tongues of fire, hear voices shouting over the screaming wind.

'I am not afraid of you,' she said carefully. 'But I am afraid for you.'

'Why?'

She took a deep breath. She had never told anyone before; never put the nightmare into words.

'I keep having this dream, this night-mare,' she said, hardly audible. 'It is the day of my father's death. He has put to sea in the "Reah", his new boat. The squall blows up suddenly and the seas are mountainous, tossing the boats about like toys. I feel the weight of water crashing over my head as if I am in the sea too, and icy coldness paralysing my limbs. The waves are huge, black, racing towards me like monsters.

'Then I see a man in the water, quite near me. It's a younger man, not my father at all. He looks at me with a startled, troubled look as if he does not know why he is there or has lost the thread of something. Then a huge and tumultuous mountain of seas comes crashing down on his head, completely obliterating him, and I see him being sucked under, drowning, and I feel as if I am suffocating with the man as he drowns...'

Her face was wet with tears. He lifted her off the rug and cradled her in his arms. He held her closely, his lips against her hair. She shut her eyes and lay against him, aware of the warmth and hardness of his body and the tangy scent of his skin.

'And the man in the sea is me?'

'Yes. Always.'

'And you didn't know me? Had never seen me before?'

'When we met at the foot of the stairs on the last day of the summer term, I recognised you as the man in my dream. It was the most shattering experience; to discover that you really existed, that you were a living person, not just a face that I imagined in a dream.'

'There must be an explanation,' said Ewart. 'I don't believe in premonitions. Perhaps you had seen my photograph in a magazine or newspaper?'

'I don't know,' said Reah wearily. 'I don't want to think about it anymore.'

He stroked her hair as she lay against him.

'Tell me about the day that your father died. Tell me what you did.'

'It was a Friday in February. A grey day with an overcast sky but no wind. My father sailed in all weathers but he had not planned to go out that day. I went to college as usual. I remember reminding him about the week-end shopping. He teased me, saying that as there was nothing left in the housekeeping he would have to go fishing for our supper.'

Her voice dropped. 'I'll never know if he went fishing or not. They never found the "Reah". A squall blew up in the afternoon, all along this stretch of the coast from Eastbourne to Shoreham. There was a lot of small shipping in difficulties. Then I learned that my father had gone out and hadn't returned.

'I stood on the cliffs looking at the pounding seas and I knew in my heart that he would not return. But I kept on hoping. He was such an experienced sailor. He'd sailed in storms before and across the Atlantic. Eventually I came back to the cottage and waited.'

'What did you do while you were here?'

Reah made a short, strangled sound. 'Heavens, I've no idea. I suppose I made a cup of tea. I put the television on, hoping there might be some news. Then someone from the lifeboat station phoned me to say that another boat had seen the "Reah" suddenly overturned by an enormous wave. It was tossed into the air like a piece of flotsam. When they looked again, for they were hard pressed to keep themselves afloat, the "Reah" had gone.'

Reah shuddered at the painful memory and Ewart's arms tightened round her. She was staring into the fire.

'I don't know how long I sat here, unbelieving. The next I knew it was sometime in the middle of the night. The television was a flickering, blank screen, the fire had gone out and I was so stiff with cold I could hardly move.'

'Then you began to have this dream?'

'I dragged myself upstairs to bed but I didn't sleep much. This dream kept coming over and over again...it was terrible.'

Reah buried her face in her hands to shut away the haunting pictures. At first she did not even hear Ewart's voice urgently asking a question.

'Reah, tell me the date of that Friday. When was it?' He had a slim diary in his hand. 'Was it the sixth of February?'

Reah looked at him wonderingly through her tears and nodded.

'Listen Reah. On the sixth of February this year, I did a live interview on television. You say you sat watching television that evening. You were in a state of shock so it's not surprising that you don't remember what you saw. It was my first appearance, and very unnerving. But what I do remember,' Ewart went on, 'is that the programme was interrupted a couple of times with news flashes about the seas battering the south coast and the lifeboats putting out to search for a famous yachtsman.

'The news flashes took us by surprise.

We were completely thrown. That startled face you saw, as if I had lost the thread of something was me all right.'

He gripped her arm firmly. 'Don't you see, Reah? That dream of yours is not wholly a dream. It's what you saw unconsciously on television that evening, as you sat here shocked and alone. You saw news shots of the turbulent seas, then me caught off guard in the studio, and somehow the two pictures have been spliced into one. That's how your dream began. It's no premonition, my darling, merely a television fantasy, a trick of the screen...'

Reah longed to believe Ewart's explanation. If only this was true, then the terror would fade. His face was close to her, his arms strong, his eyes gentle; it was a moment of sweet comfort.

'You mean, my memory cells stored the television scenes in my brain, but somehow got them all mixed up,' she said with a slow, tremulous smile.

'It sounds odd but shock can play strange tricks. I could get the recording of the programme...'

'No,' said Reah quickly. 'I couldn't bear to see it. I prefer to believe you.'

Her head was in the crook of his shoulders as a deep ache pulsed strongly through her veins. It was a feeling that almost deprived her of her senses. She felt heady with an overwhelming relief and love for Ewart. To know that there was a reasonable explanation for her dream, to know that he was not responsible for the way she had been treated by his agent...she could feel her love for Ewart growing with every heartbeat.

He led her upstairs, their arms entwined. With gentle fingers he took off the tapestry skirt and antique blouse and wrapped her shaking body in a cotton robe. He carried her to the bed and Reah clung to him, not wanting to let him go. He took off his jacket and shirt, lay down beside her and she crawled into the warmth of his arms.

His mouth travelled down her satiny skin, tasting the sweetness, feeling the smooth flesh, sending flames of desire through her slim body. She was tired, so tried but the desire was stronger. She moaned as his mouth moved against her lips, his tongue touching the inner softness, drawing her closer till she could hardly breathe.

He tangled his fingers in her dishevelled hair, gathering her against him with desperate urgency. Her body cried out for his touch, and as if he heard, his fingers began a sweet exploration of her softly swelling breast. It was a moment of ecstasy. Reah arched herself against his hand, amazed at the response surging through her body.

She whispered his name as he stroked this throbbing curve, slowly rising to the hardening tip. Her last barriers were crumbling, longing for more of the delight he was bringing to her burning flesh.

He covered her body with his own and she could feel his desire growing. It seemed she was floating in a sensation so erotic that she wondered if this, too, was all a dream. The brush of the soft hair on his chest sent her nerves tingling; she longed to bury her face in its dark curls. His bare skin drew her fingers as she began her own tentative voyage. She heard him groan as the unexpected touch triggered a powerful surge of emotion in his loins.

His face moved down her shoulders, mouthing the skin with gentle kisses as if he were tasting her. He reached her breasts and found her rising to meet his mouth. As his tongue circled her nipple, she gasped aloud. An electric shock ran through her body, both delighting and terrifying her with its strength.

They were crushing each other, aflame with the heat of this growing, unstoppable passion. Their minds were linked into an enveloping desire to merge, to become one, wanting to belong.

Her body began to tremble as his movements quickened, becoming expert and probing. Her breath was a sob as she fought to control her mounting feelings. His marvellous body was silhouetted for a moment, like a Florentine statue...he was her David...his masculine beauty a further joy to her overwhelmed senses.

There was no more time for thoughts

beyond the compelling movements which convulsed through her. She lifted her body towards him and he took her with a swift, sweet gentleness that almost shocked her with its suddenness.

Waves of pleasure rippled along every nerve, growing, surging, till Reah felt she would die with the unbearable urgency. Her whole body was out of control She did not know where she was in the darkness, what she was doing, only that a deep primitive need wanted fulfilment.

She twisted and turned, moaning, crying his name, her cheeks wet with tears. His nails gripped into her flesh but she felt no pain. His breath was hot and gasping against her mouth, seeking to bring them together to the point of no return.

Suddenly a deep shuddering groan stabbed his body. Reah felt a second of despair, of panic, but her own fiery pinnacle was not far behind. It, too, took her by surprise as the surging exploded and waves of release flooded into every limb, taking her through a plunging universe that spun with shooting stars.

NINE

The pillow beside her was empty. Ewart had gone. At some time in the early hours he slipped away, not wanting to compromise her in a small community. The Alfa Romeo was too conspicuous to be left outside her cottage.

She stretched her arms and legs, a long luxuriant movement that made her limbs tingle. A great burden was lifted from her mind. Ewart had broken the nightmare into bearable images.

And Reah had wept for the first time in months. She had cried in his arms and he had not tried to stop her, letting the tears wash away some of the pain.

Her thoughts lingered on their love-making. It had been a revelation, sheer joy, their two bodies in perfect harmony. He had not said he loved her and yet every kiss, every touch seemed to convey

215

that message. His aggressiveness had gone, arrogance disappeared; he had treated her as a beautiful and desirable woman.

In Florence Ewart had taken care of her as he promised Miss Hardcastle. She wanted to believe that this meant something. Her heart lifted.

Retrieving the shawl after her evening at the disco had been touched with moments of sheer magic, dancing with him on the deserted disco floor wearing his socks.

Reah remembered his strong hands gripping her, his passionate kisses. His cruelty had been in words, clever lines, products of his fertile and active imagination.

'But you're not going to rule my life, Ewart Morgan,' she said aloud. 'I'm not that meek.'

She longed to see him again, to be part of his life. They could work together. She sighed at her fanciful dreams, knowing that she did not belong to his world.

When the roses came to the door, Reah was immediately transported back to the flower market in Florence. They were yellow roses, of course. Ewart had not forgotten. There was a card with the roses. It said:

'Thank you for the coffee. I could become addicted.'

Reah buried her face in the yellow petals. Their perfume was delicate and English, quite different to the robust scent of their Italian counterparts. He could become addicted. It was a one-liner from a professional television dramatist; nothing more.

Her restlessness overflowed into the afternoon. A grey rain-laden sky made her feel apprehensive. When she found Ewart's silver birch stick hidden away in a cupboard in her tote bag, the impact of that first meeting returned. She held the stick, half laughing to herself, half fearful; how little she had known then. Ewart had brought a passion into her life which would be difficult to tame.

She knew a walk would clear her mind of these confused thoughts, so she put on some strong shoes, a jersey and her Trilby hat. She took the trail path through the

National Trust land; to be part of its remoteness and scenic beauty would be calming.

The background of bird chatter came from the nesting wildfowl on the lakes; dandelion clocks blew in clouds across the salt marshes and meadows like early snow; the river meandered along the estuary, free flowing and clear.

Reah loved walking on the old grasslands; the tiny blue chalkhill butterflies were chasing each other in pairs across their vast playground. In the distance the sheer chalk and flint cliffs of the virgin sisters rose from the rock shore...Haven Brow, Short Bottom, Short Brow, Limekiln Bottom, Rough Brow, Rough Bottom, Brass Point...Reah smiled at the names, a litany of her childhood and echoes from the Middle Ages before the Black Death wiped out the local farming community.

Cows and sheep grazed on the banks of the river and a single yellow canoe paddled towards the sea, the ebbing tide taking it out to Cuckmere Haven. It was a favourite area for canoeists.

Reah began to climb the steep slope using the terracettes as footholds. Her breath came fast as she pushed herself to climb the first sister in record time; from shingle shore to three hundred feet in three minutes. It was exhilarating.

At the top, she surveyed the view around; the strong wind whipping at her clothes, her ears humming with the sound. From here the sea looked smooth, shimmering with weak sunlight that was breaking through the clouds. The canoeist was a mere yellow blob, paddling determinedly. Ewart was down there in the coastguard cottage, working on his play.

It was in the air that Reah first sensed the storm. What had been a still grey sky moments before was on the move. She strained her ears, listening intently, and detected a different note. It came again, a long long way off...the low faint rumble of thunder.

She hesitated. If it was coming inland, she would not want to be caught out on the hills.

She noticed white flecks below where

earlier the sun had been dancing on the waves. The sea's colour had changed, darkened; all the blue had vanished into the depths. There was not a sea bird in sight, not a single fulmar or herring gull on the wing.

This decided Reah, only just in time. The first drops of rain fell as she began the tricky descent. It was too steep and slippery to hurry. She was going to get wet.

Suddenly the storm hit the land. The force of the wind almost knocked Reah flying. She gasped, struggling to her knees, clutching at a tough crop of tor grass. She stuffed her hat into her waistband and using both hands moved crab-wise down the chalky path.

Lightning flashed vividly in the sky over the Seven Sisters; loud cracks of thunder erupted deafeningly overhead; the rain wiped out the distant sea view.

Reah hurried downwards, slipping and sliding the last few yards to the barbed wire fence. She wanted to get away from the cliffs quickly. They were unstable and the rain could loosen the chalk.

It would be quicker to reach the shelter of the coastguard cottages. She ran along the shingle, the rough waves cutting irregular patterns in the glistening pebbles, rock pools and runnels forming beneath the onslaught of the incoming tide. The rain blew hard and needle-like against her face.

When Reah reached the flood bank, it was already too late to wade across to the other side. The tide was racing in on the current, blown by the storm and moving up the estuary in a relentless formation of white-topped waves. She stood, panting. She had come all this way for nothing. The cottages were so near, just across on the other bank, a little way up Short Cliff.

Two figures came out of the cottages. One was the coastguard in glistening oilskins; the other she knew at once was Ewart. They were running down the concrete path that led to a small sandy shore, pulling a boat out from under the cliff and dragging it down to the sea edge.

Reah gasped as she realised their

intention. They were putting out to sea in the storm.

'No! Ewart! Come back,' she shouted the wind tore her words away and tossed them into the air. She knew why they were going. The canoeist was out there in his frail yellow craft; a boy in a yellow life-jacket. Ewart would have seen him from his desk.

She ran alongside the channel, calling and waving, but the men did not hear. She heard the phut-phut of the engine as the boat slipped into the sea, almost immediately bucketed and tossed about by the waves.

'Ewart...' she cried, her voice an agony of despair. She watched the boat head to sea, the mist and rain swallowing it as if it had never existed. The sea was taking the other man that she loved; she knew she loved Ewart.

Lightning flashed across the sky with pronged streaks, stabbing the dark clouds. A crack of thunder followed immediately and violently, jolting Reah out of her dazed horror.

She must get help. She ran back to the trail path already awash with water, stumbling over unseen ruts. In some places she could not even see the path and found herself floundering near the edge of the mudflats, half blinded by the stinging rain, in league with a ferocious wind that took Reah's breath away.

The storm did not frighten her, but she was scared of losing her way among the salt marshes and mudflats of the estuary. The tide was racing in, driven by the wind, and the trail was disappearing fast.

That fear was caught in her greater fear for Ewart and his companion somewhere out in that tempestuous sea. Their boat would be like a toy on those mountainous troughs.

She was chilled to the bone, gathering all her strength to reach the inn at the entrance to the trail. She had to telephone the lifeboat station to tell them that the men had put to sea.

The mist was thickening, throwing Reah's sense of direction. She panicked, and began to run, stumbling, gasping, her feet often ankle deep in the surging water, not just rain but waves. The tide was coming in faster than she could run.

Her own danger suddenly struck her. No one knew where she was. She could just disappear, sucked under by the mud.

Wet feathers brushed her face and she screamed. The bird flapped its wings and veered off into the darkness taking strands of her hair in its claws.

When she pitched into the wooden entrance stile, she almost collapsed against it in relief. She knew where she was now, near the road. Lights loomed through the rain. Where there were lights, there would be people...telephone, cars, help...the norm of civilisation which had not existed in the last ten minutes.

'Please, help. Someone help,' she cried, rapping on the door of the inn.

The door was open and she fell inside, a wild-eyed drenched creature, muddied to the knees, her red hair plastered to her skin.

'Get the lifeboat,' she gasped. The faces at the bar were just a blur. 'Please telephone. There are two men out in a boat and they need help.'

'This lass is all but done in,' said the innkeeper putting down the glass he had been wiping. 'Get her a brandy, Mabel. Steady now. I'll telephone the lifeboat station though I reckon they've already been called out in this storm.'

'They went to rescue a boy in a canoe,' said Reah, shivering.

'Where d'you say this boat is?'

'They put out in C–Cuckmere Haven, near the old coastguard cottages. Please hurry.'

The innkeeper shook his head. 'These heroes. We never run short of heroes. I'll get onto them right away. Now you drink this before you catch your death.'

A glass was put in her hand and she drank obediently although her stiff fingers could hardly hold it. Someone guided it to her mouth. It almost choked her, fiery and heart racing. Mabel drove her home. Later the police called to tell her that the lifeboat had been called out several times in the storm; that Ewart Morgan had reported his sighting of the boy in the yellow canoe, but there was no sign of any of them. No news at all.

She sat huddled in front of the fire, her clothes still wet and steaming on her. She should have known that Ewart or the coastguard would have telephoned before putting out to sea. They were both sensible, responsible people.

Reah was living her nightmare now. The familiar cottage was no comfort. Ewart...Ewart...without Ewart there would be no point in living...anywhere.

Her heart ached with numb misery. She could have borne the knowledge of him taking another woman to that Alpine meadow, however hurtful that might have been. But he would have been alive, living, loving, giving. He would be somewhere, breathing, working, taking his full allotted span even if it was with some other woman.

She could have lived with that agony; learned how to live without him.

But if he died...she saw his face so clearly; those dark granite eyes, that taut profile, the soft fringe of hair. She did not want to be part of a world that did not hold him.

How long Reah sat in the gloom, she had no idea.

Time had no meaning. She was hardly aware of the door opening; it was only the coldness of the draught on her already chilled body that made her turn. A dark figure filled the doorway.

'Ewart?' she whispered.

'Reah...darling.'

They were in each other's arms, clinging fiercely, unable to speak, the relief of being together was enough. There was no need to kiss. The kisses would come later. They were overcome with the joy of finding each other and knowing without a doubt that they cared.

'Ewart...' Reah sobbed against his wet cheek. 'I thought you were never coming back. I thought that you had drowned and that I would never see you again and you would never know that I love you.'

'I am here. Don't cry,' he soothed. 'Nothing can part us now. Never again.

We are together. But...tell me again.'

Reah looked up at Ewart, her eyes warm with hope. She saw his strength and gentleness.

'I love you,' she said. 'I love you so much.'

'Darling girl, at last!' His voice was impassioned. He flung back his head as if unable to bear the joy. 'I always thought you were too proud and too independent to love anyone, let alone me, an arrogant writer, whom half the time you acted as if you hated.

'When I've loved you to distraction almost since that first day when you lost your hat over the cliff!'

'Me?...I?' Reah was incoherent, bewildered. 'You hardly showed it.'

'I've been running away, scared out of my wits. Scared of losing my precious freedom, afraid of being caught by a skinny young woman with red hair. When I dashed off to Milan, I was running away from you.'

Reah drew back from him so that she could see his face. His eyes were blazing down at her; the fire ignited a warm throbbing glow in her veins.

'You were running away from yourself,' she said.

'I know. I was an idiot. We were both blind. Why do you think I've been coming to your rescue so often? I've spent hours, days, worrying about you. I couldn't bear to let anything harm one hair of your dear, impetuous head. I wanted to take care of you all the time—and you wouldn't let me.'

'Of course not,' said Reah, but the softness of her voice belied the words. 'I can take care of myself. But what can I do if you go out to sea in s-storms, when I love you so much. I didn't want to live if you...if you had...'

He brushed his mouth gently against her lips to stop the torrent of anguish.

'No more tears, Reah. I'm safe and so is the boy. The lifeboat picked us up about a mile from the shore. The engine of the small boat was swamped with water.'

'Promise me you'll never do anything like that again,' she cried, gripping his arms. 'Promise me.'

'You know I can't make that kind of promise, Reah,' he said. 'Besides, who was running a one-woman marathon against the tide? You could have just as easily been hurt.'

'I knew what I was doing,' said Reah, defending herself. 'I've known the estuary since I was a child, which is more than I can say for you.'

'There was no way I could watch that boy being carried out to sea and do nothing. We are not the kind of people to tie each other down with pointless promises. Our marriage won't be a bonded cage but something gloriously free. Loving and trusting each other will be its strength.'

'Marriage?' Reah looked at him with a growing happiness. 'Is the famous Ewart Morgan actually suggesting marriage?'

'Not suggesting...stating. We are getting married. But I'm not going down on my knees in these wet clothes. You're frozen! It's time we both got out of our clothes and into the tub. Does this antiquated cottage possess a bathroom?'

'Of course,' said Reah shyly. 'There's plenty of hot water. You go first. Did you say marriage?'

'Yes, I did. I mean it. And don't look so alarmed,' he chuckled. 'I've already seen you in the bath, remember?'

Reah found herself blushing but that memory was crushed into oblivion as Ewart's mouth came down with a burning kiss that took her breath away. She flung her arms round his neck and pulled him closer, her slender body pressing against the hardness of the man she loved. She wanted him so dreadfully.

Their bodies caught alight with desire. Ewart began to peel off her wet shirt, his fingers seeking the tiny buttons without hesitation. Her bare shoulders were pale and satiny in the half light.

'How I adored you that night in Florence, so long ago, when you stood there wrapped in a ridiculous sheet, making your declaration of rights. You were wonderful. I wanted to tell you then that I loved you, but would you have believed me?'

'No,' said Reah. 'How could I, when

you had just tried to rape me. There was no love in you that night.'

He was touching her shoulders gently, lightly. She turned her head this way and that, moving under his touch.

'Perhaps not. Love and hate are very closely entwined. You were driving me wild. When I saw you with that young Italian, I went insane with jealousy. I wanted to make you mine...at any cost.'

'The cost was almost too high, my darling,' said Reah.

'I have a beautiful moonlight dress waiting for its owner to claim it,' he smiled. 'Also a green thing with slashed sleeves. Do you always leave your clothes all over the place? You'll have to stop that habit when we are married.'

'So you have them...I had been wondering.' It was becoming almost impossible to talk as their kisses deepened and grew more intense.

'And I have a sketch of the head of David, given to me by a talented young artist as a protest. Perhaps one day she'll sign it. I'll have it framed, and it will hang in the study of our home so that neither of us will ever forget Florence.'

'We'll never forget Florence,' Reah sighed.

'You're beautiful Reah...so beautiful,' he murmured.

He kissed the hollow of her throat, his lips moving over her skin with sensitive probing; she could feel her body becoming weak with a longing to be loved. Waves of sweet elation carried away her last doubts. She loved him and wanted to be loved.

'Ewart darling,' she whispered. 'Love me, love me now...'

'This time nothing is going to stop us,' he said, his dark eyes glinting. 'We are together and the door is locked against the outside world. It's still raining and no one can even see in the windows. It's you and I all the time in the world.'

'I can't think of anything I'd like more,' said Reah touching his face with infinite tenderness.

'I'm going to carry you upstairs and make love to you until you fall asleep in my arms, full of sweet content and happiness,' said Ewart. She could feel that the desire in his caressing mouth was barely restrained. She knew that when his passion was unleashed, it would be like nothing she had ever known before.

'It sounds...wonderful,' she said breathlessly.

'It is wonderful,' he said. 'And no one is going to interrupt us. I'm going to make sure of that.'

He leaned away from her momentarily. The dark hair on his chest was still glistening from the rain. He reached for the telephone and took the receiver off the hook. A faint buzz came from it; the engaged signal was in for a long session.

'But supposing Miss Hardcastle tries to telephone me,' said Reah, trying to sound shocked.

'I've a feeling Miss Hardcastle would approve,' said Ewart.

He lifted her up in his arms, their mouths clinging, hair tangling, skin tingling, their senses drowning...but drowning in a sea of love.

'To bed, my darling...' he said.

'It's not an Alpine meadow,' said Reah.

'Oh, but it is,' said Ewart. 'Can't you smell the flowers?'

The publishers hope that this book has given you enjoyable reading. Large Print Books are especially designed to be as easy to see and hold as possible. If you wish a complete list of our books, please ask at your local library or write directly to: Dales Large Print Books, Long Preston, North Yorkshire, BD23 4ND, England.

This Large Print Book for the Partially sighted, who cannot read normal print, is published under the auspices of

THE ULVERSCROFT FOUNDATION

THE ULVERSCROFT FOUNDATION

. . . we hope that you have enjoyed this Large Print Book. Please think for a moment about those people who have worse eyesight problems than you . . . and are unable to even read or enjoy Large Print, without great difficulty.

You can help them by sending a donation, large or small to:

**The Ulverscroft Foundation,
1, The Green, Bradgate Road,
Anstey, Leicestershire, LE7 7FU,
England.**

or request a copy of our brochure for more details.

The Foundation will use all your help to assist those people who are handicapped by various sight problems and need special attention.

Thank you very much for your help.